Praise for Jerry Izenberg

"When *Field of Dreams* meets *Back to the Future*, you have a wondrous tale of the Negro Leagues and its America as only Jerry Izenberg can bring to life."

— Robert Lipsyte, former columnist *NY Times*

"This is a story about baseball of the special sort that was played for decades by the men we call Negro leaguers. Go read about a love story that will grab you in your heart and make you laugh and sometimes leave you with tears. Thank you, Jerry Izenberg, for all the love you have given me in *Damn You, Josh Gibson*."

— Larry Hogan, author and Black baseball historian

"Jerry Izenberg is the dean of historical baseball writers. He knew many of the men he writes about. This gives him unique insights into his subjects. A must read."

— Leonard S. Coleman, Jr., former President of the National League

"The heroes of Negro League baseball, where Black stars were segregated before baseball integrated in the late 1940s, take over an old ballplayer's dreams and send him and his grandson on a magical tour of their times. Jerry Izenberg combines his own voluminous history of Black baseball with the compelling writing style that has made him a nationally known sports columnist. The novel's point is for young Jeffy to 'be the messenger,' to retell the story of these forgotten heroes. Hope he does as good a job as Jerry has."

— Jim Overmyer, author of *Queen of the Negro Leagues: Effa Manley and the Newark Eagle*

Damn You, Josh Gibson

A Ghost Story

Jerry Izenberg

Also by Jerry Izenberg

Nonfiction

Larry Doby in Black and White

Baseball, Nazis and Nedick's Hot Dogs: Growing Up Jewish in the 1930s in Newark

Once There Were Giants: The Golden Age of Heavyweight Boxing

Rozelle: A Biography

Through My Eyes: A Sportswriter's 58-Year Journey

No Medals for Trying

The Jerry Izenberg Collection

Championship: The NFL Title Story

How Many Miles to Camelot: The All-American Sports Myth

New York Giants 75 Years

The Greatest Game Ever Played

At Large With Jerry Izenberg

The Rivals

Great Latin Sports Figures

Fiction

After the Fire: Love and Hate in the Ashes of 1967

Contents

*For three remarkable friends who enriched my life: the late
Monte Irvin, the late Larry Doby, and the late Max Manning.
They played this beautiful game more for joy than money.*

Foreword

In 1954, Jacques Barzun, a French-born philosopher caught up in a serious love affair with the America in which he lived and taught, wrote, "Whoever would understand the heart and mind of America had better learn baseball, the rules and realities of the game."

He was legitimately trying to explain the American psyche through its love of a game that can generate magnificent beauty one moment and communal despair the next.

Decades before Barzun wrote that, there was another side of America that felt the same love and despair from the beautiful game, although that side was totally excluded from its highest level.

The men who played it had been barred from so-called organized baseball and its major leagues. But it was played under the same rules. Like in mainstream America, its bases were ninety feet apart and its games were nine innings in length. Like mainstream America's game, the ball was white.

But none of the players were.

They were all African Americans, forced into an athletic subculture of their own by the ugliest of America's shames: racism.

Because of it, the Negro National and American Leagues were born. So were America's separate but at the very least equal baseball heroes. As a result, the majority of America's baseball fans never saw Josh Gibson hit a 500-foot home run or Cool Papa Bell score from second on a bunt or pitchers like Smokey Joe Williams and Leon Day or hitters like Turkey Stearnes or great teams like the Kansas City Monarchs, the Homestead Grays, and the Pittsburgh Crawfords.

The obscenity of racism turned them into shadow dancers, performing in limited obscurity in their own country. Because salaries were low and the league seasons short, the men who played in these segregated games became knights of the open road, following the sun at season's end to Mexico and Puerto Rico, to Cuba and the Dominican Republic, to Venezuela and anywhere else men of color were allowed to play the game that was so much a part of their lives.

The doors to Major League Baseball were seemingly forever barred to them, but bitterness never tainted the purity of that love affair. They were baseball men, playing the game they were born to play.

And the ultimate irony of those games was that in those venues—unlike in the land of their birth—they were no longer black men playing baseball for primarily black audiences. They were instead baseball players playing in front of crowds that never gave even a thought to their skin pigmentation.

In the Mexican League, for example, the cheers for Monte Irvin, an African-American, dwarfed by far those heard for Mexican-born heroes. And the further irony was that in those Latin winter leagues, they often played side by side with white American-born players who at season's end returned to the segregated major leagues of the United States.

"It was sort of accepted by us because we didn't have the time to brood about things we had no power to change,'" the late Max Manning, a pitcher for the Newark Eagles, once said to me. "We grew up with it, and we were too busy playing the game we so loved to wonder why."

Monte Irvin and Larry Doby, two superstars who did move from the Negro Leagues to the majors, each told me that Max was good enough to be a starting pitcher on almost any major-league team but never got the chance.

"Some folks said that it [the whites-only rule of Major League Baseball] cheated me out of the best years of my life," Max said. "Maybe it did, but I'll go to my grave knowing our game [black baseball] was pure. There wasn't any money in it, so it didn't change our thinking. We didn't play to prove things to others. We played to prove things to ourselves.

"We sang on the buses, and we didn't mind that once in a while we played three games in one day. We were doing what we wanted to do, playing the game we loved. Our seasons never ended. When the schedule ran out, most of us followed the sun and played more baseball in countries most Americans never got to see."

There are those who still deride the achievements of Negro League stars because, as a Veterans Committee member of the National Baseball Hall of Fame once said decades ago, when none of these guys were even mentioned as Hall of Fame candidates: "We had nothing to go on. They kept very limited statistics."

"They wanted us to keep better statistics?" Irvin, a Negro Leagues veteran, color-barrier-breaker with the New York Giants, and legitimate Hall of Famer, once asked rhetorically. "What does that mean? Hell, they didn't even want us to play the game."

To say their credentials were unverifiable is like saying Miles Davis was just a trumpet player, Arthur Ashe and Althea

Gibson just played tennis, and Paul Robeson and Billie Holiday just sang songs.

So it was for these Americans who played America's game, but almost always within the framework of a strange form of American apartheid.

Sometimes I wonder who was cheated more: these baseball knights of the open road, or the white America that loved the same game with the same intensity but hardly ever got to see these men who played it as well as or better than anyone else.

With that said, on a fine September day in 2007, near home plate at Newark's Bears & Eagles Stadium, the idea for this book began. More than an idea, it was really a command performance. I was the MC at an event honoring fifteen players from Newark's professional baseball history, more than a century old, who had later been inducted into the Baseball Hall of Fame in Cooperstown, New York.

One of them was Irvin, who was 88 years old. He had been a standout on the Negro Leagues' Newark Eagles, a hero on two New York Giants' World Series teams as the first African American to play for that franchise, and an administrative aide to the commissioner of baseball. He and I talked after the ceremonies.

"I want you to know," he told me, "that you can't die. I really mean it. Don't die."

"I'll try to stay alive," I said.

"Listen, what I mean is, you can't die, because you are the last writer to see us play in the Negro Leagues. If you go, who will tell people about us? I mean, the kids won't even believe our leagues ever existed."

And that was the impetus for what became this book. Jeffrey Jefferson was not real. Once upon a time, the three ghosts were, but that was a long time ago, and obviously they did not collaborate with me.

But beyond that, every tableau they created for Jefferson's grandson was real—every single one of them, as was every single person recalled within their framework. Understand that, and you will understand exactly what Monte meant that day, and what far too much of America missed.

So, Monte, this is all about keeping that promise.

This is for you and those too often forgotten men who lit up the past, and, most of all, for the majority of Americans, young and old, who never were blessed enough to see them do it.

Jerry Izenberg
January 6th, 2026
Henderson, Nevada

Chapter 1

"Goddamn You, Josh Gibson"

T he old ballplayer was dreaming again, as he did more and more lately. In the dreams, he played in many different stadiums. This time he was in Santa Clara, Cuba, in tiny Boulanger Stadium. It was 1937, and he knew where he was because just beyond the outfield walls he could see the familiar ring of tall palm trees. In the dreams, he wore the uniforms of many teams. This time his gray visitor's jersey bore the name "Habana" stitched across its front in navy-blue script.

The venues were always different. But the dream was always the same. He could hear the crack of the bat, and as he turned his head he could see the great Oscar Charleston—who in the summers played against him in the Negro Leagues—circling under the towering fly ball, and could feel the weight of his back foot pressed against the base as he prepared to push off as soon as he heard the third-base coach yell, "Go, go, go!"

Then, as always, in every single dream, he was no longer old. Instead, the legs that stole bases in hundreds of stadiums year after year were flying toward home and, as always, the big body crouched low to guard the plate was the same. Josh

Gibson was waiting for him. But this time, caught in the euphoria of the dream, he was sure he would get there.

He slid.

And then it was all gone.

Suddenly, there was only the sound of the clock radio kicking in with the voice of WNJR disc jockey Georgie Hudson:

"Get movin', all you nine-to-fivers, or you're gonna be late for work. So while you take that last swallow of coffee before you head out the door, here's Frankie Lymon and the Teenagers with a musical thought for the day: 'Why do fools fall in love?'"

The old ballplayer's left arm snaked out and ferociously slammed down hard on the "off" button. "They fall in love because they're fools, fool," he mumbled at the now-silent radio. Then the familiar throb in his left leg, which he'd come to call Josh Gibson's Revenge, hit him full force, as it did every morning.

He half-rolled, half-slid out of bed. When his left foot hit the floor, spears of pain shot up his leg, and he shouted toward the ceiling as he limped toward the bathroom, "Goddamn you, Josh Gibson, goddamn you! I'm sixty-three years old, but I slid into so many bases that I got the knees of an eighty-two-year-old man. But I can live another sixty-three years with this pain and smile, because it won't change one damn thing. I was safe, and you know it."

The old ballplayer's name was Jeffrey Jefferson Jr., but in another world, when he was young and life was beautiful, they called him Jeff the Jet.

In the summers, he roamed the outfield for the Negro National League's Newark Eagles. But before and after each season he was a baseball nomad . . . a knight of the open road who, like all the others who were denied access because of their skin color to what the white world called organized baseball, followed the sun to Cuba and Puerto Rico . . . to the Dominican Republic and Venezuela . . . to Mexico and any other place on the planet where the rainouts were few, the days and nights were warm, and he could keep playing the beautiful game.

Even now in his mind's eye, he could see an afternoon at Newark's long-gone Ruppert Stadium that forever shaped his life. He was inching away from first base in a half-crouch, weight balanced to go either way, fingers flexing like a metronome keeping time with his concentration, and shouting over at the Homestead Grays' Ray Brown on the mound, "You can throw that curveball all day long, but I won't see it because on the next pitch I'll be gone!"

And the crowd joined the challenge—13,000 of them on a sun-drenched Memorial Day, with a full-throated chant:

"Go, Jet . . . Go, Jet . . . Go, Jet!"

And after Brown failed to pick him off twice, he went.

He stole second. And the chant grew louder.

He stole third. And the chant became an all-out roar.

Now, he would steal home. He could recall that last tableau as though it were yesterday. He saw Josh Gibson shove the right-handed batter aside as though he were a rag doll. He saw that big body blocking the plate like a concrete barrier just as the old-man-now-younger lived the dream again, artfully twisted his body, and went into a hook slide, leaving nothing between him and Gibson's desperate lunge except a corridor of air. The big catcher blew the tag, but his body came crashing down directly on Jet's leg, leaving it twisted and shattered.

He looked up and saw the umpire, who must have had the vision of an overaged bat, pump his right fist with the thumb pointed skyward, and he heard a single sound echoing like a cannon shot above the dust:

"Yer out!"

And then his leg began to throb. It hadn't stopped throbbing since.

He had finished shaving when the sounds of what had become the traditional morning battle between his daughter and his grandson drifted back from the kitchen.

"I told you," said the mother, who never lost this fight, "no Devil Dogs. Too much sugar. You got a peanut butter and jelly sandwich and a big red apple for dessert. That's gonna be your school lunch, and you ain't gonna win this or any other argument with me."

"Aw, Ma . . ."

"Don't you 'aw, Ma' me. I gotta get to work. And don't you roll your eyes at me. You pick up that sack and your book bag before you miss the bus. And if you're late again and I have to come to school, Lord help you—because your grandfather can't.

"And I surely do mean that," she said to the old ballplayer, who had walked into the kitchen.

"Hey, girl, kitchen closed for breakfast? And before you get started, lower your voice, please. I got the miseries again this morning. Old Josh Gibson pullin' at my leg right now like he's in a tug-o'-war with the devil."

Behind her, he could see little Jeffy trying not to laugh.

"Ain't nothing wrong with you," she shot back, hiding her own smile, "except that you're gonna make him late for school. Sit down. I fried you a couple of eggs, there's bacon, and you can put the toast on yourself."

The harsher she sounded, the more he knew it was an act of love, just like the way her mother had handled him.

The girl's name was Effa Jefferson. She had been named after Effa Manley, the co-owner and general manger of the Newark Eagles. The first time he saw little Effa, she was wrapped in a blanket in her mother's arms at the hospital. Jefferson had asked his wife, Barbara, "What should we name her?" And Barbara, who knew she had married a baseball lifer, simply smiled and said, "She needs a baseball name. Mrs. Manley has done so much for us—we'll call her Effa."

Years later, when Effa bore his only grandchild, she took charge, just as her mother had: "We'll call him Jeffy—after the greatest ballplayer I ever knew."

As Effa gave her father orders in the kitchen, Jeffy wiped his smile away. He looked at the man, whom he obviously adored, and said, as he did every morning: "Pop Pop, I hate old Josh Gibson.'"

"I know, son, but best you hold on for a minute—you are talking about the greatest hitter who ever lived. I do recall that one time . . ."

"Oh, please, no," Effa said. "Not another story."

"Hush, girl, 'cause you might learn something, too. Now, I remember a time we was beatin' his Homestead Grays, 3-1, up in Pittsburgh. Ninth inning. They had two men on and two outs, and as I recollect, Max Manning was pitchin' for us.

"He tried to cut a curveball just a little too fine and he hung it, and old Josh caught it right on the sweet spot. He hit it so hard and so high that it disappeared. Guys were running around the bases, and the ball never did come down. And that's how we lost the game.

"Next day in Newark, we're playin' them again. Just before the game starts I'm on the third-base line and I'm passing the time with one of the umpires. Suddenly I look up and damned if I don't see a baseball falling out of the sky. So I run over and catch it. And that umpire, he whirls around and points to the Grays' dugout and hollers, 'Gibson, you're out—yesterday in Pittsburgh!

"Only time I ever got the better of Josh. Now get on outta here, boy, and let me eat breakfast because I got places to go, things to do, and people to see today."

Chapter 2
"Who Will Tell the Children?"

The house was quiet now. The sun streamed in through the kitchen window, and he sat there with both hands around a second cup of coffee. The cup was old and chipped, a gift from his late wife, and he liked to look at the writing in big white letters on one side:

"Go, Jet, Go"

Barbara had bought it and had it lettered during a second honeymoon trip they took to Atlantic City after the Eagles had won their first Negro League World Series in 1946. Someone else would have chosen something like "I love you" or "My hero," but Barbara understood what she had opted for when she chose him. He was a baseball lifer; the words she chose for that cup said just about everything about the base-ball man she had married and the lifestyle they shared for so many years.

He could still conjure up the images of that special day in Atlantic City as if it were happening again. All of it: the wooden boardwalk, the sunlight dancing off the ocean, the waves rolling toward the shore. He could hear the beach sounds of young people at play and the nonstop calliope from the Steel Pier. He breathed in deeply and he smelled the sticky-sweet aroma of caramel popcorn from a store of candy treats across from the boardwalk benches.

Alone with his memories, he heard her giggle, and in his mind's eye he saw her playfully reach up, lift his navy-blue baseball cap with its big white script "E" on the front, and place it on her own head. He remembered that in that instant he touched a lock of her hair, peeking out from under the hat, the same one he'd worn in what the newspapers had called the Colored World Series in September that year. Pain had yet to leave its mark on her young face. Cancer had yet to attack her body. He had always believed this was the single most beautiful moment of his entire life.

He could almost hear himself think (or was he actually saying the words out loud in the empty kitchen?), "Lord, if this is a dream, don't let me wake up. Let me be with her again. Let me stay . . ." But the reverie vaporized, leaving him only with the pain in his left leg.

When the all-white major leagues had begun to integrate, he thought for a while that because he knew the Negro Leagues so well, maybe the Giants or the Yankees or the Dodgers would hire him as a scout. He would have been good at it, too. Or maybe, with integration, he could have been a minor-league manager or a major-league coach. To wear what had always been an unobtainable uniform might have taken some of the sting out of what was destined to become the dream forever denied that marked the cadence of an incomplete life.

He would really have liked to grow old doing that. But nobody called. In his heart, he knew he would have worked like hell trying to travel from sandlot to sandlot, scouting kids, sometimes in three games a day, while the pain Old Josh had left him hampered his mobility.

Now, the only baseball he saw live was the high school and

semipro games he could walk to over at West Side Park. His daughter knew he would be there every afternoon there was a game. He didn't know how she found out about the high school kids who would stop by and sit in the stands for an inning or two and make fun of the stories he told about the way he had played in a league they were sure had never even existed. He told them about "Double Duty" Ted Radcliffe, who caught all nine innings of the first game of a doubleheader for the Pittsburgh Crawfords in 1932 and then went to the mound and pitched a shutout in the second game. He told them how Willie Wells, a shortstop and later manager for the all-black Newark Eagles, got so tired of pitchers throwing at him that he bought a hard hat from a construction worker and wore it in the batter's box.

"And that, young men," Jet said, "was the first batting helmet in baseball history."

None of them believed a word he had said. The kid who seemed to be the ringleader snatched his cane, and the three of them taunted him as they played keep-away with it, laughing and imitating him until, for reasons he never knew, his daughter appeared, gave them hell, and threatened to call the park policeman nearby, who she said was her cousin. A lie, but they didn't wait to find out. They took off running and didn't come back.

"You wanna go home now?" she asked him.

"What I want is for you to stop acting like you're my mother."

But he smiled with his heart as he said it. This girl, he thought, is very much her mother's daughter.

He liked the way she was raising Jeffy, and he felt as though the private talks they had at night and the way Jeffy looked at him were adding years to a life that had begun to fade from the moment the only woman he'd ever loved had died.

His daughter and his grandson kept him going—them, and his love affair with baseball. His daughter was his safe haven in a world where he continued to seek the sum total of all that had been and all that almost was in a lonely life that always seemed to add up to "coulda, shoulda, and mighta."

But as close as he was to the daughter who looked so much like her mother, he never—but absolutely never—told her about the ghosts.

One night, he admitted to her that he had prematurely begun to forget things; it scared him, he said, when he thought about what that might mean. She listened quietly, and when he finished she reached across the kitchen table and gently put her hand in his and promised that no matter what happened to him in the years ahead, she would never put him in a home. He would always be with her and the boy. He believed her.

Nevertheless, he kept his silence about the ghosts. It would be asking too much for her to understand about them. Hell, how could she, if he didn't understand them?

He looked at his watch. There was a game today; time to go. He took his cane from the umbrella stand next to the front door. It was a heavy mahogany African walking stick that an old Cuban fan had given him outside Gran Estadio de La Habana the night he stole home against Cienfuegos. He called it Martin, after Martín Dihigo, a winter-league teammate on Los Rojos del Habana. The day his daughter told him she didn't like him walking down South Orange Avenue alone at night, he laughed. "Don't you worry about me. What I can't handle"—he brandished the cane—"old Martín Dihigo damn sure can."

And he proved it one night when three gang kids surrounded him and one of them opened his bomber jacket, revealing the olive-drab butt of a Glock .22 pistol. Looking into the kid's cold, dead eyes, he instinctively knew with certainty that this man-child could kill him with no thought at all. The kid grinned and grunted, "Get up off that wallet, old man, or you're a dead old man."

A single unspoken thought leaped from the back roads of his mind: "I'm old, but I ain't dead just yet." His left hand crossed underneath his right, and in a single fluid motion born in decades of batter's boxes past, Jeff Jefferson swung old Martín Dihigo as though he had just gotten the green light on a 3-0 fastball.

The kid went down with a shattered jaw. His scream was part agony, the rest disbelief. The other two ran. An hour later, his daughter walked through the front door of the West District precinct house and let loose.

"I told you a million times this was gonna happen!" she yelled. "How many times do I have to—"

"Hi there, Princess, what brings you out this late at night?"

And then he laughed.

"It's not funny, Daddy! You could have . . ." She paused. "Oh, hell . . ."

Then they were hugging.

He recalled that night as he stepped outside and locked the door behind him. He limped down the old-fashioned stone steps and headed across 13th Street. It was April, but New Jersey takes its own good time about surrendering to the calendar, so there was still a chill in the air, and his leg hurt, and he knew who to blame. About ten muttered "Goddamn you, Josh Gibson"s later, he pushed open the door to Siegel's Candy Store, at the corner of 13th Street and 16th Avenue.

The store was empty of customers. He hoped the old man, not his kid, would be there. He found no warmth in the kid, but in Jet's "other world," Abe Siegel had worked a concession stand at Ruppert Stadium, sometimes even walking up and down the concrete steps to hawk his wares. He was maybe fifteen years older than the old ballplayer and was already middle-aged when the Jet was a rising star. Back then, whether it was the all-white Newark Bears of the International League or the all-black Newark Eagles of the Negro National League, for Abe the meaning of Ruppert Stadium was always the same —a nonstop mantra heard in every ballpark from Maine to California:

"Red hots . . . red hots . . . get ya red hot dogs . . . Co' beer, ice co' beer . . . scorecards, ten cents."

The skin color of the crowd didn't matter. The skin color of the players didn't matter. Without giving it a thought, Abe was actually the advance guard of successful baseball integration long before Jackie Robinson and Larry Doby grabbed the game and pulled it kicking and screaming into the 20th century, from which it was hiding.

Abe was the old ballplayer's last surviving link with his youth. Abe's candy store was often Jet's social club, his debating society, his private confessional.

Abe was the only one he ever told about the ghosts.

"Hey, boychik!" Abe hollered from behind the soda fountain counter. "You're slowing down, man. Expected you an hour ago. Saved you a *Star-Ledger* sports section. It's West Side-Central today. I like that little Puerto Rican pitcher Central has. You seen him play yet?"

"He's okay, Abe. A little small . . . needs more muscle if he's gonna throw a real fastball. But he's got some style." Then his expression changed—his smile was gone as he gazed at the old man. "I can't take it much longer, Abe. You know what I mean —seeing those ghosts every damn day. Are they real?" He shook his head slowly. "I'm scared, Abe. I don't dare tell anyone but you about them. Am I slipping into . . . well, I read something about dementia the other day. Abe . . ." He paused, lowered his head. "What am I going to do?"

Abe set two cups of coffee on the counter and wiped his hands on his apron. He gestured: "Sit, Jet, for a minute." He poured too much sugar into his coffee, stirred it gently. Then he put the spoon down and stared in silence toward the street for a full minute. Jet, alongside him, waited. He leaned forward.

"Abe . . ."

"I'm getting to it, Jet." Abe cleared his throat. "If you think you saw ghosts, you saw ghosts. The thing is: Why?" He turned back toward the window, then abruptly shifted his gaze to the old ballplayer's eyes. "You know I wasn't always a vendor at the ballpark. I did a few things in my time that weren't so good. I drove for the boys from Newark on a few jobs. We made some money. Some people got hurt—a lot of people. And some got . . . well, you know what I mean.

"I think what we do at any age becomes a part of us forever. I'm old, Jet. I don't see no ghosts at my age. What I see when I'm trying to fall asleep at night ain't ghosts. What I see"—the old ballplayer watched the old man lean back into his seat, his eyes misty— "is my own private devils. My dad called them dybbuks in Yiddish. And they ain't pretty or forgiving. I learned to live with that.

"So now you got to live with whatever put its footprints on your past. What you're seeing depends on what you did. Personally, I don't believe you got anything to be ashamed of. I know you. You lived a straight life. You were a hell of a ballplayer, and I know the best of the best in your league respected you. Maybe your ghosts ain't so bad, boychik. Maybe they just need or want something from you . . . something they can't do for themselves. Something that, for some reason, only you can give them.

"But you can't help them or yourself unless you calm down, take a breath." He smiled. "Hysteria will make you meshugga."

Jet slammed his cup down so hard that coffee flew. Then

the fear and desperation seemed to pour out, and it was directed against the only person he could confide in.

"I confided in you!" he shouted at Abe. "I came to you for help, not this bullshit." Jet glared. "I shouldn't have told you!" he barked. "You shouldn't have answered if that's the best you can give me. I thought you'd have learned at your age that you can't bullshit a bullshitter. Can't you see I'm drowning? Forget I ever said anything! Forget it."

He stormed out, yanking the door hard behind him. He limped up 16th Avenue toward the park. It was huge—thirty-six acres in all—shielded on this side by a stand of maple and elm trees between the baseball field and the street. He turned onto a well-worn path that snaked through the foliage, came out next to the cement bleachers, tossed his cane onto the bottom step, and pulled himself up.

High school baseball lacks the glamour of a Saturday football game; no bands or cheerleaders or other trappings. Today the stands were virtually empty except for a handful of parents and girlfriends, which is the way the old ballplayer liked it. He was free to concentrate.

The game was already in the third inning, and the little Puerto Rican left-hander's team was locked in a scoreless tie. The old ballplayer liked the way the pitcher went about his business, calm, seeing only the catcher's target with a studied confidence.

But he really had no fastball. He was getting by on junk and control. He needed to develop two more pitches to impress a scout if he wanted to be a serious prospect.

The batter had the look of a miscast linebacker: broad shoulders, thick neck, wide Roy Campanella-like stance. He was clearly more athlete than baseball player. He swung twice with more muscle than skill and missed each time. The little pitcher had run the count to 0-2.

"Now he's got to work the corners," the old ballplayer thought. "Now the batter has to protect the plate. If he fools him with the corners, he's got him." The pitcher-batter battle never changes. It's as old as baseball itself, and at 0-2, the pitcher held all the cards.

From the first row of the bleachers, the old ballplayer could see the batter's face; he knew from the set of his jaw and from the slight tremor in his biceps that the pitcher had this one won. The batter would swing at anything now. All the pitcher had to do was . . .

But he didn't.

He threw another junk pitch straight down the middle. From the sound of bat hitting ball, the old ballplayer knew it was gone.

"Home run on an 0-2 pitch . . . disgraceful," Jet thought as he watched the hitter trot past first base, turn toward second . . . and then . . . and then . . . the world froze. The dark-blue sky turned white. The horizon turned white. The faint sunlight went ice-cold. The scattered applause from the tiny crowd began to fade until it was no louder than the hum of a mosquito. The images on the field blurred in front of him and morphed into a fuzzy slow motion. His head began to ache.

They were back.

No background . . . no foreground . . . just the three of them in uniform. Josh, bigger and broader by far than the other two . . . Satchel Paige, whose uniform seemed to change colors like some eerie slide show, because he played for at least twenty teams from here to the Dominican Republic . . . and Leon Day, an old Eagles teammate, wearing Newark's home white.

At first, as always, they didn't speak. They just stood there, filling the frame of his surreal vision, staring him down the way Leon used to stare down a hitter. The old ballplayer began to shiver.

Their silence seemed to penetrate his very core. "What do you want?" Jet yelled. "What the hell do you want from me? You're dead. I know you're dead. I went to Leon's funeral. This is the sixth damn visit from you. Say something!

"Look at my leg, Josh. You turned it into a glob of wet spaghetti. Damn you . . . all of you . . . What the hell do you want from me?"

And then, for the first time, Josh seemed to float a half-step forward. Jet recoiled involuntarily. The big man tipped his Homestead Grays cap as though he were acknowledging yet another home run to a packed house. Then he threw his head back and roared—the same derisive laughter Jet had heard that day at home plate in Newark when the umpire called him out and Josh taunted him while the bolts of pain ran the length of his left leg and Jeffrey Jefferson Jr. knew he would never again play the game he loved.

And when the laughter stopped, the eyes of the man some say might have been the greatest hitter who ever lived seemed to fill with pain. Josh Gibson leaned even closer and in a voice half-demanding and half-desperate, he spoke:

"Who will tell the children?"

Just that single sentence.

And then there was nothing.

The three apparitions were gone, vaporizing as suddenly as they had appeared.

The old ballplayer shouted after them: "What do you want from me? What children? Why are you doing this?"

The sky turned blue again. The baserunner triumphantly reached home plate and celebrated with his teammates. The noise of the scattered crowd drifted back to him. The little left-handed pitcher was waiting on the mound with the catcher for the coach to come get him.

The old ballplayer trembled. He shook his head, bent

down, retrieved his cane. He stumbled, fought for his balance as he climbed down from the bleachers.

Was he going mad? Had they really been there? Was he senile? He thought of Abe's words: Maybe they wanted something? But what the hell was it? He stumbled again. He was simultaneously enraged and frightened.

He limped home. He did not stop at Siegel's Candy Store. And just before he turned the key in the lock, he looked up at the sky, shook his fist, and yelled, "Goddamn you, Josh Gibson!"

Chapter 3
Home to Where the Heart Was

All that night, it was as though the ghosts had never left. Each time he closed his eyes, desperately seeking sleep, the all-too-vivid memory of them hammered away at his psyche. The booming laughter of Josh Gibson returned to assault his ears. He was caught in a mental vise between fear and disbelief. He was sure of what he had seen and heard in the park that afternoon . . . but he also knew that death is death. It was against everything in which he believed—his life experience, his religion, his common sense— to acknowledge their appearance.

But he could not deny that he had heard Josh's question, with its accusatory demand for an answer:

"Who will tell the children?"

All night, he sank deeper and deeper into a pit of emotional quicksand, struggling to see the line between what he believed to be fact and what he knew to be fantasy. But Josh's demand continued to resonate through the web of his half-sleep:

What children . . . where . . . how?

All his life he had been an initiator. If he wanted to steal second base, he went and did it. If he thought he could nail the runner heading for home, he ignored the cutoff man and got him. If a pitcher tried to back him away from the plate with a blatantly inside fastball, he got off the ground, brushed the dirt from his uniform, and crowded the plate even more.

But now he was being asked—ordered—to react. Now an enigma so convoluted he could not even begin to understand it was pressuring him to be the reactor, not the initiator.

He lay there in the darkness and stared at the plastic blinds as the light seeping through them morphed from dark gray to orange-tinted sunrise. With the sight of dawn's early light, the old ballplayer surrendered. The silent clock radio beside the bed read 6:12. He edged cautiously out of bed, and as he slid his feet into his worn old slippers, Josh Gibson's Revenge awakened with him and sent a jolt of pain down the length of his left leg.

But this time he did not invoke his reflex response. He did not mutter "Goddamn you, Josh Gibson." Instead, loudly, clearly: "What am I going to do, Lord? What can I do?"

It was Saturday. His daughter had worked all week at the hospital's oncology floor, surrounded each moment by suffering and pain and not-so-quiet desperation. He didn't know how she could do it. Tomorrow morning was church day. But this was Saturday; they'd agreed she had earned the right to sleep as late as she could.

Today the boy was his responsibility. He limped into the kitchen, took down two cereal bowls and spoons from a cabinet. Then he limped back to his bedroom, opened the bottom dresser drawer, and pulled out a box of Froot Loops hiding beneath his polo shirts. His daughter had banned the cereal, along with some others: "Too much sugar. You gonna pay to fill all those cavities?"

He once told Jeffy, "We got one day a week to ourselves.

One day. We can choose our own cereal. Don't you worry, it's our breakfast. Ain't hers."

By the time Jeffy appeared in the kitchen, Pop Pop had poured the milk, made the toast, and rehidden the secret cereal.

"Hey, Pop Pop, Yankees and Red Sox on TV today from Boston," the boy said between spoonfuls. "You ever play against the Red Sox?"

"Not likely, young man. We not only played in different ballparks, we played in different worlds back then. But I did play in Yankee Stadium twice, against Josh and the Grays and against Satch and the K.C. Monarchs. Didn't get no hits but walked twice and stole two bases off Satch. Made a pretty nice throw against the Monarchs to catch Buck O'Neil at home plate, too."

As the boy finished his cereal, he smiled at the old ballplayer. "I wish old Josh Gibson didn't mess up your leg, Pop Pop. I'll bet you'd still be playing and then I could see you steal a lot of bases."

Jet smiled ruefully. "I know I cuss his name now and then. But, young man, never forget what I am going to say now. It was an honor and a privilege just to play on the same ball field with him. A lot of young fellas in the major leagues today couldn't have earned that right."

Jeffy nodded, then thought for a few moments. "So what are we gonna do today? It's our Saturday."

"Well," the old ballplayer said, "I thought you could finish breakfast and then you could get the baseball gloves out of my room and we could go to the park and play us some catch this morning and watch the Yanks and the Sox later. Maybe after lunch we could go spend a little time with Uncle Abe."

The boy threw both arms in the air. "Yay, Uncle Abe. Yay, banana splits from Uncle Abe."

The old ball player laughed, then threw his own arms in the air. "Yes indeed. Banana splits from Uncle Abe."

They were still laughing as they exchanged high-fives.

That afternoon as they crossed 13th Street and turned toward 16th Avenue, the boy said, "I don't understand, Pop Pop, how you can talk about Josh Gibson the way you do when he messed up your leg. Besides, if he was such a great hitter like, say, Hank Aaron or Willie Mays, how come I never heard anyone ever call his name but you?"

"Well, that's tricky. Seems that when a white major leaguer retires, he . . . gets better in folks' minds every five years, and after twenty years people think he's a Hall of Famer. But when a Negro Leaguer is gone, well . . . he's just gone. I guess . . . well, hell, I gotta say that's one question I can't answer. Kids today never even heard of the Homestead Grays or the Pittsburgh Crawfords or the Newark Eagles."

He stopped and looked down at the boy. "But you have."

They had reached Siegel's store. As they entered, the old ballplayer clapped his hands twice. "Do I smell banana splits?"

At the end of the counter, the mother of the little Puerto Rican pitcher who had thrown the home run ball the day Josh's ghost finally spoke to him was negotiating her daily numbers buy with Abe. At a single genuine-fake white marble table near the back, a teenage boy and girl were sharing an ice cream soda with two straws, never losing eye contact.

The old ball player smiled. "See those two?" he said to the boy. "Forty-five years ago, that would have been me and your grandmother."

The pitcher's mother and Abe had finished their transaction. Abe sent her on her way with a warm, *"Buenos dias, señora."* He wore a white waist-high apron, a white shirt, and a thirty-year-old navy-blue Newark Bears cap with a white "N" on the crown.

"Well, well, look who's here, boychik and boychik III," he said as he approached. "I can't imagine why you're here on a Saturday after lunch. I could guess banana splits, but I know that this guy"—he gestured toward Jeffy—"doesn't like them, and—"

"I like banana splits, Uncle Abe," the boy cut in. "I love banana splits."

"Then why am I over here?" Siegel said with a big laugh. "I got to get up there and make a couple."

When Siegel returned and served the ice cream, the old ballplayer said, "Jeffy, why don't you go to the newsstand over there, pick up a Sports Illustrated, and look through it at that counter while you eat your ice cream?"

The boy picked up his magazine and sat at a counter stool with it and his ice cream. Abe came back with his ubiquitous cup of coffee and sat across from Jet. "Well, how you doing with them dybbuks? Beware of the ones disguised as females—especially if they have big chests."

"Not funny, Abe," the old ballplayer said. "I'm going through hell."

Jet raked his spoon across the vanilla ice cream in front of him, then dropped it and folded his arms. "Abe, I didn't sleep last night. Not at all. I couldn't. I kept thinking about who's going to tell these mysterious children, the ones Josh mentioned —his only words. Another thing I can't figure out, can't piece it together. And Jeffy has me thinking about things I haven't thought of in years. On the way here he asked me why people can talk about Willie Mays and Hank Aaron but he never hears anyone talk about Josh or Satchel or any of my guys." He unfolded his arms as his body slumped forward. "He's right, you know."

"Not surprising," Abe said. "It's thirteen years since the Eagles left this town. Seventeen years since you guys won the

Negro Leagues World Series. Hell, it's sixteen years since Jackie broke the major-league color line. There ain't been a baseball team, black or white, in this city since 1950. If Jeffy didn't live in your house, he wouldn't know who Josh was either."

Abe stopped, shook his head. His face took on the look of a man in mid-epiphany, a man who had just learned the answer to a great riddle. He turned and pointed to Jeffy.

"You see that little person over there demolishing his banana split? Well, he don't look like no senior citizen to me. He is a sure-enough certified child. And I'll bet you he never heard of Mule Suttles or Judy Johnson or Turkey Stearnes. If you weren't his grandfather"—Abe pointed a gnarled finger at the old ballplayer this time—"he never would have heard of Jeff the Jet either. Knowin' all this, I'm thinkin' your ghosts are starting to make a little sense to me."

"Do you mean, uh . . ."

"Hey, he's a kid, ain't he? Monday, the Greater Newark High School Baseball Tournament starts over at Ruppert Stadium. Lots of memories in that park for you and me . . . the Yankees' Newark Bears, your Eagles, my hot dog stand. All gone now. Like us, just history waiting for the last chapter. Now it's just an old shell waiting for the wrecking ball to finish the job. Kinda like . . . no, just like you and me.

"But I got to say," Abe went on, "well, if I was a baseball ghost who played in this town, that park just might be where I'd be hangin' out. I think"—he paused, raised an eyebrow, and poured his gaze into Jet's—"that just might be the place where your ghosts would like to meet your grandson."

Abe turned toward Jeffy, who was trying to unearth one last spoonful of ice cream from the bottom of his dish. "Hey, boychik III," Abe hollered, "how'd you like to go to a baseball game on Monday with your grandad?"

"Really?"

"Really. He wants to introduce you to some old friends there."

The old ballplayer started to say something, then stopped. "We'll see," he told the boy. "But now we got the Yanks and Red Sox on television, and we gotta move it."

Outside on the sidewalk, the old ballplayer put his arm around his grandson's shoulder and looked toward the sky.

"We're gonna try, Josh," he murmured. "We're gonna try."

It was as much a prayer as a statement.

LATER THAT NIGHT, THE OLD BALLPLAYER DID SOMETHING he hadn't done in years. He rummaged around in the bottom of his closet, pushed aside his three pairs of shoes, and pulled out a big cardboard box covered by a thin film of dust. He brought it into the kitchen, where Jeffy was listening to the radio.

"What you got there, Pop Pop? Something for me?"

The old ballplayer smiled. "I guess you could say I been savin' this for you without even knowin' it. With some of the things I been seein' lately, it's time for me to show it to you."

A piece of the brittle cardboard tore away when he opened the top. He reached inside and pulled out a large five-and-ten-cent-store scrapbook. Years before, the old ballplayer had taped a piece of notebook paper to the book's red cover. Scrawled across the paper: "Property of Jeff Jefferson, who was once property of the Newark Eagles Professional Baseball Team."

The old ballplayer and the young boy leaned over the table together. Jet picked up the book and handed it gently to his grandson.

The boy flipped the cover open. On the first page there was

a yellowed old newspaper photograph: a collision at home plate.

The baserunner was on the ground with his left leg doubled under him. The big catcher had sprawled on top of it. The caption read, "Eagles outfielder Jeff Jefferson out at home against the Homestead Grays at Ruppert Stadium yesterday as Josh Gibson applies the tag."

The boy, wide-eyed, looked up. "Is this the . . ."

"Yes, it is, son. And after that play I never played another inning of baseball. It hurts a little to look at it." Jet lowered his head. Then he laughed. "But not as much as my goddamn leg hurt when that picture was taken."

He pointed at the book. "But turn the page—there's a lot more I want you to see."

They leafed through it together . . . through a montage of faded pictures and clippings that formed the first tangible evidence the boy had ever seen of the incarnation that was his grandfather's life long before the boy was born.

Now the boy had faces to put with the names that the old ballplayer conjured on nights when bedtime stories began with, "Did I ever tell you about the time we played this exhibition game against Josh over in Pennsylvania, and he hit a ball five hundred feet, out of the park, across the street, through a living-room window, and the mayor of the town said, 'Nobody is gonna believe this, so will somebody please go across the street and get me that ball?'?" . . . or, "Did I ever tell you about the Opening Day in Newark when Leon Day was pitching a shutout for ten innings but we didn't score either, so he stood on the dugout steps with a bat in his hand in the bottom of the tenth, and said to us, 'I guess I got to do this all by myself, don't I?' and then went up and hit a home run to end it?"

They were all there, with many more, in that ancient scrapbook, looking back at the boy. The boy wished inwardly that once, just once, he could have seen the old ballplayer performing miraculous feats.

Then the old ballplayer said to the boy, "Turn the page—I want you to take a good look at this ballpark, because—" and an envelope fell out onto the table.

"Well, well. Open it, boy."

And there was a photo of a young woman sitting in a front-row seat by the low green wall that separated the foul territory of a playing field from the third-base seats.

"That's your grandmother, son, the one you never saw," the old ballplayer said softly. "Isn't she beautiful?"

The boy held the picture in his small hands. He gazed. "She looks just like Mommy."

"Yes indeed," the old ballplayer said, his voice softening more. "She surely does."

He carefully replaced the picture in the envelope and pointed to the last page of the book. It was one of those typical ballpark photographs taken from behind home plate and looking out toward center field. The boy could see "410 feet" painted on the distant fence.

"That's Ruppert Stadium," the old ballplayer said. "That's where I hit my first professional home run—into the bleachers in left-center . . . Where I stole my first base . . . where years later I played my last game."

"It's big," the boy said, almost solemnly. "I've never been in a baseball stadium that big."

"Yeah, it was big in size, and even bigger in my life. I met your grandmother there between games of a Sunday doubleheader. And she took your mom to see your granddad play there. For me, it was . . . well, it was home.

"But you'll see for yourself tomorrow. It ain't pretty like it was. The bleachers are gone, and, like me, I guess it's kinda old and worn. But a high school game is there tomorrow, and that's where we're gonna be."

The old ballplayer flashed a big smile. "Now you better get to bed before your mom catches us."

The boy was so excited it took him a long time to get to sleep.

It took the old ballplayer even longer.

Chapter 4
You Can Go Home Again

They walked over to South Orange Avenue and took the #31 bus, just as the old ballplayer had done each time the Eagles had a home game at Ruppert in that other slice of his long-gone world. He dropped the fare into the toll box and let the boy run to find a window seat.

It occurred to him as he settled into a seat that he and the boy had never had occasion before to ride the #31 bus together. Each time something caught Jeffy's eye through the window his excitement showed, but the old ballplayer rode in silence.

He watched with mixed emotions as the landmarks of a journey that once was routine to him glided past: the Strand and Congress movie houses (soon to be abandoned) . . . the County Court House with its world-famous statue of Abe Lincoln looking benevolently toward Springfield Avenue . . . to the downtown intersection of Newark's busiest area, known locally as the four corners at Broad and Market Streets.

The bus cut across Broad to where Market merged with Ferry Street, and then to the ballpark, two blocks from the elevated Pulaski Skyway that connected Newark and Jersey City.

The old ball player hadn't taken this ride since seventeen

years ago—the Memorial Day collision at home plate, when he had limped away from baseball forever. In truth, this was a journey he did not want to make. He did not want to tear away the emotional scabs time had formed over painful old wounds. He did not want to be reminded of the way his wife had run down the aisle behind the home dugout, where the players' wives sat, and tried to scramble over the low cement wall between the seats and the field to get to him, lying on the ground under Josh. He remembered the fear in her eyes as she held his hand in the ambulance. And although he had tried for what seemed like a million times, he would never forget the moment when he asked the doctor if he would ever play base-ball again; the doctor had paused, then slowly shook his head: "No. And don't even try it if you want to walk again."

The stadium was the last stop on the #31 route. A high school baseball game wasn't enough to fill the bus more than halfway. The old ballplayer and the boy walked slowly to the corner along with a few other fans and turned toward the ball-park two blocks away.

As they walked, the old ballplayer conjured up the joy of Sunday baseball in the Negro Leagues when the Yankee farm club was on the road and the Eagles took over the park for a doubleheader.

"On Sundays, they always came right after church, like they did in the other cities in the Negro National League," the old man said. "And, boy, you should have seen how fine the women looked in their Sunday-go-to-church dresses and the men with their ties and jackets and most of them even wearing fedoras. Once I'd found your grandmother . . . those were the happiest days of my life."

Just ahead, they saw the half-razed stadium coming into view but it seemed to him as though the earth had shifted and the skyline tilted until he realized that the light towers, installed here even before most major-league teams had lights, were gone—sold for scrap.

Suddenly, he knew what was eating away at him during the bus ride. He knew that most of all he dreaded seeing how greed and civic neglect had turned the repository of his youthful dreams into an eroding mausoleum.

He was in no way prepared for what he saw. Except for the name "Stadium Auto Wreckers" painted on a junkyard wall beyond the left-field fence, not a single landmark remained along Wilson Avenue.

The front facade of the stadium itself was still intact. But there was no activity on the street. He took a deep breath, squeezed the boy's hand. Together they entered the shell of what had been the grand lobby. The box-office windows were shuttered. The stairs leading to the locker rooms atop the single-decked park were rotting. Nobody dressed there. Only high school kids played here now, and they boarded their team buses in full uniform.

The pair walked up the single remaining ramp into the daylight ahead. The cruelest sight of all awaited the old ballplayer. The grandstand seats were gone. So were the outfield bleachers. Only the dugouts remained. This was the place where the Yankees' top farm club set minor-league records, the place where his Eagles represented the heart and soul of the county's black community with a constituency rivaled only by the town's jazz clubs.

But now, what was once the crown jewel of high school competitions in New Jersey baseball drew fewer than two hundred fans this day. A year later, the tournament finals moved over to Bloomfield Avenue and a football field so unsuited for baseball that balls that cleared the short left- and right-field fences were declared ground-rule doubles.

Kids who weren't even born when the old ballplayer's team

won its only Negro Leagues World Series title had been forced to play out a requiem for a ballpark that, for a city now sliding toward decay, was once much more than a baseball stadium.

It was his youth and magic and a place where hope was almost never defeated by nine bad innings. Or if it was, it always rose up the next day to give the city nine good ones. The cadence of the ballpark had been the music of the old ballplayer's life. But now the Bears were gone. The Eagles were gone. Professional baseball in Newark was gone.

The residue of a building that once measured the city's heartbeat now offered nothing but emotional ashes.

In the 1970s, a decade later, a Jersey pop singer named Melanie would sing, "Look what they done to my song, Ma." She could easily have been offering up a dirge for the loss of the city's baseball teams.

"Where are we going to sit, Pop Pop?" the boy asked.

Before the old ballplayer could answer, the question became superfluous. Preceded by a tremendous thunderclap and a jagged slash of lightning, the sky turned black and the rain came pelting across the stadium floor.

The South Side High School kids raced for their bus, as did the visiting team from Morristown. The fans scurried for cover.

The boy shivered. "What are we going to do, Pop Pop? I'm scared."

"It looks to me," said the old ballplayer, staring out toward center field, "as though it's being done for us."

In the distance, at the edge of what had been the municipal dump, 500 yards beyond the center-field fence, the darkness was gone. In its place was the biggest rainbow either of them had ever seen. Only this one was moving . . . moving through the fence . . . past the infield . . . and, finally, straddling home plate.

The backdrop of reborn sunlight behind it was dazzling.

The boy's face was pure puzzlement, but the old ballplayer knew exactly what was about to happen—it was why he had been summoned. He no longer doubted.

"We're here, Josh," he said simply.

"Who are you talking to, Pop Pop?" the boy asked.

"Where are you, Josh?" the old ballplayer said.

"Don't do that, Pop Pop!" the boy said, visibly frightened. "I'm the only one here."

And then there was a burst of pure light that only the old ballplayer could see—and there Josh was. "Right here, Jet, right here," he said. "You better find a way to tell that boy he ain't gonna see me . . . Maybe never . . . And you better do it now— we got places to go."

The old ballplayer put his arm around his grandson. "Something wonderful is going to happen. I can't tell you why or how, but it's something you need to know and never forget. You know I love you, boy, and I ain't never going to put you in harm's way. So just be patient." The boy, eyes gaping, nodded slowly.

"You always was a favorite of kids and old people," Josh whispered. "Me? I was inclined to prefer the company of young ladies."

Jet grimaced. "You didn't get us here for that," he said. "What do you want from us?"

Gibson threw back his ghostly head and laughed. He swung his right arm in a broad semicircular motion. "First, I suggest you look behind you and wave to all those people!"

"People?" the old ballplayer said. Then he turned toward the gutted grandstand. Suddenly, the Ruppert Stadium of his youth was back; the stands were packed; it could have been Opening Day or a Negro Leagues World Series game. There was red, white, and blue bunting draped over the low wall by the stands, and more of it hanging from the grandstand roof.

The Eagles, in home white, and the Homestead Grays, in their muted road uniforms, were spread out facing one another along the two foul lines. The voice of the Eagles' P.A. announcer, Jocko Maxwell, generally thought of in later years as America's first black sportscaster, soared across the diamond:

"Ladies and gentlemen, we direct your attention to the third-base side of the field and co-owner Effa Manley's box. The beautiful and talented Miss Lena Horne will throw out the first ball of the 1946 season to Biz Mackey."

Lena Horne, resplendent in a maroon dress, lobbed a looping throw to the Eagles' manager. The crowd cheered as Mackey signed it and jogged over to present it to her. The band struck up "Take Me Out to the Ball Game," the players trotted to their dugouts, and Miss Horne threw kisses to the fans, who roared approval.

"What the hell is going on?" Jet, stunned, hollered over the noise. "Where are we?"

Josh let go another booming laugh. "Smack in the middle of 1946, Jet. It's Opening Day."

"Why aren't Leon and Satch with you?"

"We'll see them later down the road, but right now we got places to go and memories to see."

The trio hustled down the dugout steps, up the tunnel, past the dressing-room staircases freshly painted for Opening Day, past the box-office windows where latecomers, who had been caught in the heavy pre-game traffic, were still buying tickets. Before they reached the street, Jet saw Abe Manley, Effa's husband and co-owner of the Eagles, grinning and joking with some of the latecomers. He wore a dark-blue suit, a flowered tie, and thin-rimmed spectacles.

"Hey, Mr. Manley," Jet heard himself say. "You lookin' good. It's me, the Jet."

"He can't hear you, Jet," Josh said. "Can't even see you. I

told you—we got rules about that. You and the boy can see everything I show you, but . . . in between, when you talk to me . . . as far as your boy there is concerned, you are talking to thin air."

Then Josh was gone.

As the old ballplayer and the boy walked out through the Wilson gate, the rainstorm that had wiped out the high school game resumed with increased intensity.

"We got to run for it, son!" Jet hollered.

"Run where?" Jeffy yelled back into the wind.

"There—there! On the corner by the players' entrance."

An old yellow school bus was parked next to the doorway. Both of its doors were wide open. The old man grabbed the boy's hand tighter as they ran through the downpour and on to the bus.

They settled side by side in twin seats behind the driver's seat.

As the old man labored to get his breath back, he looked around. "I know this bus," he said as much to himself as to his grandson. "It's . . . oh, no. Couldn't be."

"Couldn't be what, Pop Pop?" the boy asked.

"No, it's just an old man being foolish. But . . . it sure looks like that bucket of bolts the Eagles used to ride in before we won the Negro League World Series back in 1946. And, damn —look here." He pointed to the wall next to them. "Right there. Look. See those penknife scratches? That's where Mule Suttles carved his initials."

"That's because it is." They both jumped as Gibson's deep voice rumbled across the leather interior and rattled the side windows.

"This is the ghost of the bus that carried us to spring training in Florida and back up to Newark," said Josh, seated directly behind them. "My joints still ache from those rides, Jet, and so must yours. So sit back. We gonna be here a long, long time. Long enough to show this young man who we were and what we did. Long enough so that he can tell the skeptics who come afterward that we had our own major leagues and the people came out wherever we went—and to hell with Jim Crow."

Then the window next to them, on its own, rolled down. But all they could see was a heavy fog.

"Where are we? What's happening?" the boy asked.

"Darned if I know," the old ballplayer said.

"Look closer," said Josh. "See that water? It's the English Channel. See, the fog is burning off. Then you'll understand why we're here.

"All those boats down there are loaded with soldiers," he said, pointing. "This is D-Day. Before it's over, 2,500 American soldiers will die. The group nearest us is the 818th Amphibian Battalion. Their mission is to ride those boats across the channel, wade ashore through the bullets and the shrapnel, and secure a three-mile stretch on the western flank of the operation. It's called Utah Beach. That guy over there—recognize him, Jet?"

"It's Leon," the old ballplayer muttered. "You said we'd see him again."

"Who's Leon, Pop Pop?" the boy asked.

"Leon Day! I must have told you about him—if I didn't, then shame on me. He's only the best right-handed pitcher I ever played with. Probably even the best athlete I ever saw. He was so good that on days he didn't pitch, the Eagles kept him in the lineup. Pitched every fourth day. Then would play second or the outfield—and never hit below .320 for a season.

"Some folks say that even Satch realized how good Leon was after our '42 Negro Leagues All-Star game, although he never talked about it. As I recall, they both came in to pitch in the seventh with the Nationals and Americans tied at 2-2. Leon struck out the first five hitters he faced and didn't give up a run. Satch gave up three.

"Leon did it against hitters like you"—he pointed at Josh—"and Willie Brown and Sam Bankhead from the Homestead Grays, and Cool Papa Bell from the Chicago American Giants. Leon didn't talk, didn't smile. He just threw his 95-mile-an-hour fastballs and down-and-dirty curves right by them.

"Satch got all the publicity because he was a great pitcher and an even greater self-promoter. Leon didn't look for publicity, he looked for strikeouts. Held the single-game record of nineteen—in an eighteen-inning game. That was a record for our league, and maybe any other league."

As he spoke, there was a deepening roar overhead—the sky was dark with American B-24 bombers cruising by. They flew sortie after sortie; heavy smoke rose from the German positions across the channel. As the Higgins boats pushed off, the old ballplayer and the boy saw the planes drop lower in close support of the invasion force.

They saw Leon, pushing forward in waist-high water, bent slightly under the weight of the pack on his back, his rifle held horizontally over his head. They were hitting the beach in four separate waves. As they fought to establish a viable beachhead, the Germans destroyed dams and flooded the coastal plain ahead.

At the end of the day, 197 men died at Utah Beach.

The old ballplayer and the boy saw it all. And then their collective vision tunneled into a narrow focus, where they heard Leon talking to a war correspondent after the battle: "I was scared as hell. I lost a lot of good friends today."

Suddenly, the tableau slipped out of focus. Guided by some invisible force, there was only the bus. The English Channel was gone, replaced by a huge stadium in Nuremberg,

Germany . . . the same venue where Hitler held one of the biggest rallies in the history of the Nazi Party. But here, now, the war was over, and the American command had elected to fill a void for the occupying army with a gift they had not seen for years: baseball.

The old ballplayer and the boy looked at that sea of thousands of men in Army and Marine khaki and Navy-blue uniforms in the stadium. They were cheering for a pitcher who was one strike away from retiring the side.

The pitcher looked at the catcher from the mound. His face was impassive, emotionless. But watching him on a little hill sixty feet from home plate, the old ballplayer knew all about the fire that always raged in Leon Day's belly.

He didn't smile. His expression never changed. "Damn," the old ballplayer said, "that's old Leon."

He nodded in pride and the boy jumped in the air and whooped excitedly when Day fired strike three.

Josh spoke up, pausing the spell. "We gotta make another stop for Leon," he said. "There's one more chapter to his story."

As the view from the window turned dark, the old ballplayer put an arm around the boy and told him more about Leon Day . . . how his teammate, Hall of Famer Monte Irvin, called him the most complete athlete he had ever seen on a baseball field . . . about the year Leon recorded a perfect 13-0 record . . . about his final season, after he was traded to the Baltimore Elite Giants, with an arm that was dying, while he fought the inevitable as he had fought the Nazis.

Then the view from the window was filled by a large building. "Baltimore!" Josh hollered in Jet's ear.

"What is this place, Pop Pop?" the boy asked.

"The sign says it's St. Agnes Hospital," Jet replied, "so you pay attention."

Then they were in a hospital room. Leon was propped up

in a bed, talking to a man the old ballplayer knew very well. It was their Eagles teammate Max Manning.

They were discussing the fact that Leon's wife of thirty-four years had no chance at a baseball pension because the kind of people who were still running the major leagues did not have a clue about the injustices they had spawned and defended.

There were just 170 survivors remaining from the times in black baseball leagues when only the ball was white. Many of them had outlived their wives, which further decreased the pool of their widows.

"So what about Geraldine?" Leon was asking. "She's sixty-four, she lost a kidney, and she works in a warehouse as a fork-lift operator. Those bastards knew you and I could pitch in the majors. But they deliberately kept us out. And now we got no pension. We got nothing." His head drooped back on the pillow.

"Well, as I understand it," Max said, "they want to exclude any of us who were still in the Negro Leagues after 1947. On the Eagles, that includes you and me and Biz Mackey and Ray Dandridge."

"Damn," Leon said. "Only Jackie and Larry were taken in 1947. Look at all those who were left out. I'm just a dumb ballplayer, Max, but you taught school for more than forty-five years. Does it make sense to you?"

"You know who they are, Leon. And you know how they think. Then and now, to hell with 'em." He shifted his chair closer to the bed. "Let's talk about the Hall."

The old ballplayer gently put an arm around the boy's shoulders. "My old friend is dying," he heard himself explaining. "Now baseball got this special committee to pick the best of the ones they kept out of their baseball in the first place and put them into their Hall of Fame. Guess they think that makes everything just fine and all-American dandy. They're votin' on Leon today."

A nurse opened the door. She had a baseball in one hand. With her was a guy whom Max and Leon had ever seen. "Mr. Day," the man said, "I'm from the *Baltimore Sun*. I'm here to get your reaction to the news."

"What news?" Leon said.

"You've just been voted into the Hall of Fame. I have a photographer who wants to take a picture of you autographing this baseball for Miss Scott here."

"Well," Leon said softly, "I'll be damned." He gave a broad smile. "Gimme that ball, Miss Scott!" Beaming, the nurse handed it over with a pen. Leon wrote "HOF," then signed his name.

As the photographer took pictures, the reporter said, "I hate to ask this, Mr. Day, but how do you feel about being kept out of the big leagues?"

Leon smiled again. Then he winked at Max. "You're wrong about that, young man. I did play in the majors. I sure enough did. I'm not meanin' to down anybody, but I can tell you that I'm not so sure some of those white boys in their own major leagues were good enough to play in ours."

The journalists and the nurse left soon after. Leon asked Max to crank up his bed a little. He thought a bit.

"You know me, Max. I don't care much about the ceremony. I'll probably be gone by then. And even if I am here, it was proving the point that mattered. But I want you to promise me you'll go up there and make sure they tell the world about what all of us did." He sighed and lay back.

Max nodded solemnly.

Josh looked at the boy and then at Leon. "We best go now," he said. "He'll be joining me in six days."

Chapter 5
The Golden Era of Bronzeville

They shut the window—the fog was back again, obscuring everything.

"Why couldn't Mr. Day play in that other major league?" the boy asked. "And why did he think some of the other guys couldn't play in his? Who made those rules, Pop Pop?"

Josh Gibson exploded into laughter so hard he almost dematerialized. "Yeah, man, I'm sure glad explainin' that ain't my problem," he said. "Why don't you just go on ahead, Jet? I'd like to hear the answer to that one myself."

The old ballplayer looked at the boy with a mixture of love and incredulity. Then he remembered the boy was only eight years old and raised in Newark, New Jersey. The boy had never seen a "whites only" sign. He had never been in a classroom that wasn't integrated. He had never heard of his late father or his mother being deprived of the right to vote.

He also realized that the boy needed to be told so he would know how it was and why Willie Mays and Hank Aaron and Bob Gibson could play in that "other" major league but his own grandfather could not.

He leaned down, put both hands on his shoulders and

looked into his eyes. He was careful not to raise his voice in anger as the old memories raced through the backroads of his mind.

"Jeffy," he began softly, "there was a time when black people and white people in this country were separated by law. We didn't go to school together. In some states we couldn't vote. It was wrong, and it was bad. So, we couldn't play in their baseball leagues. But what that did was make us stronger in a different way. Everyone who was black—and I mean everyone—took pride in our leagues. When some white reporters called Josh Gibson the black Babe Ruth, we said that the Babe was the white Josh Gibson. I knew a lot of us would have been stars in their major league, and Leon was right when he said he didn't know if some of them could have played in ours.

"That foolishness ended when America finally started to recognize some of its past wrongs toward black folks. It happened too late for me and Leon and a lot of others to play in baseball's major leagues, but I want you never to forget these two names: Jackie Robinson and Larry Doby. They went through hell to break the color line to integrate the major leagues in 1947.

"When you get a little further along in school, you'll learn about brave people like Martin Luther King who made America understand what needed to be done. But what's more American than baseball? Some folks—and I'm one of them—believe a little bit of the change began just 90 feet from home plate in a place called Ebbets Field. That was the first time Jackie, the only black man on the field, broke for home and stole it. In that instant, the only color all of Brooklyn cared about was the color of his uniform."

The boy, listening, nodded slowly.

"Preach, brother, preach!" Josh boomed. "You fooled me on this one, Jet. Maybe you should have been a minister instead of trying to slide past me at home. Anyway, the education of this boy is gonna pick up in a hurry when you see where we are."

The fog disappeared. In front of them now was a big square building with a red-brick facade. A green awning above the entrance bore the legend "Southway Hotel."

"I know this place," the old ballplayer said. "It's on South Park in Chicago. I stayed here a couple of times when we played the Chicago American Giants in exhibition games, a few All-Star games, and when we played the Monarchs in the World Series. This place was good times."

He turned back to the boy. "We had this East-West All-Star game and every time it was played in Chicago, black folks came from all over the country for the great baseball and the nighttime high life. I had a teammate named Monte Irvin on the Eagles who used to say, 'They didn't pay us but fifty dollars for playing, and that was gone in one night. We went home without any money but with enough memories to last a lifetime.'

"When it came to good times," the old ballplayer said, more to Josh than the boy, "there was nothin' in all of baseball like Chicago at East-West time."

"Why was that, Pop Pop?" the boy asked.

"Well," the old ballplayer said, "there was a neighborhood in Chicago that was almost all black folks, sort of like Harlem in New York or Black Bottom in Detroit. They called it Bronzeville because, as you know, boy, we come in all shades, like tan and brown and black, and I guess they figured if you put them all together what you got was bronze."

"Tell him about the nightlife," Josh said. "The fine ladies we used to meet at the Savoy Ballroom. And how afterward we would . . ."

"Damn, Josh, there are some things he don't need to know just now." He turned back to the boy, and from deep within him the words flowed about the larger meaning of an All-Star week in Chicago to black folks across the entire face of America. Like Joe Louis' rise to the heavyweight championship, it was something they viewed as strictly their own.

"Bronzeville at night was like some Arabian Nights movie. There was a big theater with plush red seats called the Regal. The stage shows were more important than the movies. Everybody who was anybody in Chicago played there . . . Cab Calloway, Count Basie, Joe Williams, Fletcher Henderson.

"Visitors hit a lot of bars in Bronzeville that week. There was one called the Palm where a young local guy got his start singing. His name was Nat 'King' Cole.

"We didn't have to leave Bronzeville for anything. The two clubs that dominated socializing for East-West visitors and the locals were the Club DeLisa and the Rhumboogie Cafe. The story was that Joe Louis bankrolled a street hustler named Charlie Glenn to start the DeLisa. Glenn knew Bronzeville and the city and people well enough to make the club go. He hired a great house band led by a fellow named Red Saunders. It was an open secret that the DeLisa had high-stakes gambling in the basement—but we best leave stories about the basement out of this little talk."

"If the newspapers didn't cover the games," the boy asked, "how did everybody know what was happening?"

"We had our own newspapers, and you could buy them just about anywhere, even outside their home cities. Two of them, the *Pittsburgh Courier* and the *Chicago Defender*, helped make the East-West game happen."

"History time is over, Jet," Josh interrupted. "I think we best look inside and check out the lobby."

The Southway was a kind of unofficial headquarters for the team owners and players, as well as showbiz celebrities. It was Saturday night, the night before the game, but the crowds had started to check in on Thursday. The lobby was sardine-tight with them.

"See that lady over there in the corner?" the old ballplayer said to the boy, pointing to a beautiful light-skinned woman, dressed to the nines in a sleeveless black V-neck dress with an elegant string of pearls. "That's Effa Manley. You could say she was my boss with the Eagles. She and her husband, Abe, owned the team. He was more of a talent scout and she handled the business.

"The guy she and Abe are talking to is . . . Satchel Paige! Satch always said he was the king of all Negro pitchers, although I favored Leon, myself. But I have to give the devil his due. I didn't get many hits off him."

Just then somebody in the crowd hollered across the room toward Abe and Effa that a bunch of them were headed out to the DeLisa. Satch yelled back, "Count me in!"

"I sure would like to see the DeLisa one more time," Jet said wistfully, as he gazed at the crowd. "But I read it would be torn down in 1957."

"Never mind that now, "Josh told him. "Look who just checked in."

The old ballplayer's eyes opened even wider. "Jeffy," he said in quiet awe. "That man over there is a real American hero. His name is Paul Robeson. When he went to Rutgers, he was one of only two black men on campus. The football team didn't want him—but eventually he became an All-American. He was also a catcher on the Rutgers baseball team—some folks say that defensively he was much better than Josh."

"That's a damn lie," Josh shouted, "and you know it!"

"Hey, man," Jet retorted, "he can't hear you—like you told me again and again, you got rules! So save your breath, because I'm gonna say whatever the hell I want to say."

He turned to the boy. "Yeah, they tell me he could block

the plate perfectly—without having to break a fella's leg! He graduated Rutgers and then Columbia Law School, both magna cum laude.

"But in the end, what he turned out to be was a singer. And what a singer. If they ever made a movie and needed someone to be the voice of God, Paul Robeson would have been the only choice.

"His dad was a minister. Paul stood for the working man. He didn't care that they called him a Communist, which he was not. He spoke up against injustice—not only for our people but for all Americans, and, in fact, for all people everywhere."

Jeffy broke his thunderstruck silence. "Why is he here, Pop Pop?"

"Don't answer that," Josh cut in, "because you don't know! He'll come back again during this journey. I just wanted the boy to know who he was.

"But now," the ghost intoned, "tell Jeffy to close his eyes and count to five. We got a ballgame to see! And I don't want to miss batting practice. I want so much to see myself hit."

The old ballplayer complied. The boy excitedly closed his eyes and waited. When his grandfather gave him the word, his eyes fluttered open, then gaped.

"Wow!" the boy said. "I thought Ruppert Stadium was big, but I never saw anything like this place. What's it called?"

"This is Comiskey Park," the old ballplayer said. "It's the home of the Chicago White Sox. Built in 1910 . . . honest foul line 363 to left, 382 to right, 420 to center . . . capacity 50,000 back when we played our All-Star games here."

He inclined his head, as if listening. "Josh just reminded me that in 1943—which is where we are today!—we drew a lot more than those so-called major leaguers, many times. That man played in ten Negro League All-Star games."

The old ballplayer turned again toward Josh. But Josh had

materialized down on the field, sitting on top of the portable batting-practice backstop. He sat, feet dangling, cheering for the hitter . . . who also happened to be . . . Josh.

Batter Josh was pounding balls over the fence, pitch after pitch—bang, bang, bang. Then, just as suddenly, he was beside the old ballplayer and the boy in the bus.

"Look over there," Jet said, pointing toward a dugout. "That's Satch."

"Where are you, Pop Pop?" the boy asked, scanning the field.

"Yeah, Pop Pop," Josh shouted with a glee that Jet recognized all too well, "where are you?"

"Sorry, boy," the old ballplayer said, glaring at Josh. "I didn't make the All-Star game that season—that was the year Mrs. Manley refused to give me a raise, so I went down to Mexico to play with our third baseman Ray Dandridge."

The boy continued peering out the window at the hubbub on the field. Josh murmured to his friend, "I didn't mean to hurt your feelings, Jeff. You could really play this game. I promise it'll be all square business from here on in."

He leaned closer, and though he knew the boy couldn't hear him, his voice dropped to a whisper: "There's things this boy has to know. He's gonna be our messenger."

His voice turned husky. "Listen to me, Jet. The old black newspaper guys are dying. The people who saw our first All-Star game, in 1937, are dying. Who is going to tell the next generation of kids that we once had these leagues? And that, no matter how they denied us, we were who we were, and some of our own were the best who ever played this game?"

Josh put a ghostly hand on Jet's shoulder. "Why do you think I'm here? This boy"—his other hand pointed at Jeffy's awestruck face—"will be the messenger for all of us."

The game began. Josh produced a blue baseball cap that

had the legend "East" on the crown and told the old ballplayer, "Between your Eagles and my Pittsburgh Crawfords and Homestead Grays, he's genetically programmed to root for the East."

It was turning into the best day of the boy's life. And one of the most educational—he noticed something that owners in the so-called white major leagues didn't learn for another four years: At least a quarter of the fans in the stands were white.

When Satch went in to pitch, the boy was thrilled. Satch was showing the boy that he and the Negro Leaguers were all business as they played this game. In truth, the white major-leaguers historically treated their All-Star game as an exhibition contest, and the prevailing wisdom among bigots was that black baseball was a Harlem Globetrotters show on spikes. But Satch, at the time a member of the Kansas City Monarchs, wanted to help prove otherwise to the boy.

To the delight of a standing-room crowd of 51,723, the West team won, 2-1, and Satchel Paige was the star. He faced nine batters in his three-inning stint, struck out four and allowed just one ball to leave the infield, a lonely pop fly. As icing on the cake, he doubled in his lone at-bat—and the boy swore that Satch waved to him as he left the on-deck circle.

Finally, the scene faded. The old ballplayer turned back to the ghost: "What now?"

"Now," Josh answered, "we are going to visit a few familiar faces."

And the old Eagles' bus roared off through the years.

Chapter 6
South of the Color Line

Once again, the fog cleared.

The boy leaned forward, his arms folded on the open window. "Look, look!" he yelled. "There's mountains, Pop Pop! I never saw mountains before."

The old ball player turned to Josh. "What mountains are they?" he asked.

"The Sierra Madre Oriental," the ghost replied. "Man, just look around—we in Mexico now. This is the home field of Los Azules de Veracruz. I know you never been here before, but look yonder there. You know those two guys." He was pointing toward the hometown dugout, where one of the Azules was talking to a player from the visiting Monterey Industriales.

With a big smile, the old ballplayer said to the boy, "That's Monte Irvin and Roy Campanella. Played with Monte when I was an Eagle. And I played against Campy when he caught for the Philadelphia Stars."

"Yeah!" said Josh. "And as part of his education, you better tell the boy why they were down here in Mexico."

The old ballplayer turned to the boy and launched an explanation. "Both of them will wind up in the Hall of Fame at Cooperstown, and neither of them was getting paid decent money in the Negro Leagues. That was one thing. We had to do a lot of scuffling for money. If we had a family, we had to jump at the few opportunities to put a little more bread on the table. Biz Mackey was a great player as well as my manager on the Eagles the year we won. He was the catcher in an East-West All-Star game at the age of 51. And after the Eagles' seasons were over, he would drive a cab in Newark."

He paused. "If you didn't go out on the road and play winter ball, you had to hustle.

"Take Monte over there. He wanted to get married to his childhood sweetheart. But he was makin' only $150 a month. For a player of his stature, that was pretty insulting. He asked Mrs. Manley for $25 more per month—not per game, per month. And she said she couldn't afford it. That was 1942. He had to leave the Eagles, and his home in Orange, and come down here—for $25 a month. When he got here, all he did was bat .397 and hit twenty-nine home runs. Led the league with both.

"Money was tight for all of us. Now, here in Mexico with Campy, it wasn't the money. Every move he made reminded you how much he just wanted to keep on doin' what he was doin'. But, yeah, a lot of the best in the Negro Leagues did come down here for the money. Guys I played with or against: Willie Wells . . . Cool Papa Bell . . . Ray Dandridge . . . Leon Day Double Duty Radcliffe . . . just to name a few. But I think Campy had other reasons.

"Campy was the guy who once described the players in our leagues as having the best of both worlds because, he said, 'They're paying us for playing a game we'd play for free.'"

The old ballplayer paused for breath. He pointed to a man in the first row of box seats near home plate. "That fella," he told the boy, "is the reason for it all. His name is Jorge Pasquel. We're in 1942 in this scene! He owns four of the Mexican

League's six teams. In four years he'll get twenty-three white boys from the majors and the high minors to jump to his league and scare hell out of the major-league owners. But right now, he's bringing the best from the Negro Leagues to Mexico. His league failed in the end. But it was the first serious step toward integrating all of the game.

"Another man who wanted integration was Bill Veeck. Later in 1947, weeks after Jack Robinson broke the National League color line, Veeck signed Larry Doby to be the first black player in the American League for his Indians.

"Boy, talk about scaring the white power structure. Monte told me that in 1943 Veeck had a plan to buy the bankrupt Philadelphia Phillies and stock the team with guys from the Negro Leagues. He later told Monte he was gonna sign Paige and Wells and Ray Dandridge and Buck O'Neil, to name a few.

"They say when Kenesaw Mountain Landis, the commissioner, found out, he made a call to Philadelphia. Later that day, the Phillies' owner sold his team to a guy named Cox for half of what Veeck had offered. When Veeck told the guy they already had a deal, the guy laughed and said, 'So sue me.'"

"So why didn't you play down here?" the boy asked.

"Ha!" the ghost cut in. "You gonna tell him the truth—that nobody asked you to that party?"

"Listen, big mouth, that ain't the way it was and you know it," Jet shot back. "It was because I had just signed a new contract with Mrs. Manley, and unlike you I valued my word more than money." He quickly explained that to the boy. "And meanwhile I hope you're watching this game, boy," he added, pointing toward the on-deck circle, where Irvin was kneeling. "We're in the ninth and Veracruz has the potential winning runs on base and . . . whoa, wait, where is Monte going? Why is he walking over to Pasquel's seat?"

"No problem!" Josh said with a chuckle. "Close your eyes, count to five—and you'll be able to hear what everybody in this stadium says. Better yet"—his smile deepened—"I'll also pick up what we ghosts call 'future-speak'!"

And then the scene shifted again—to a newspaper office in Newark, thirty years in the future. Monte Irvin was telling a columnist what happened that day:

"He called me, so I go over," Monte was saying. "He put his arm around me and looked in my eyes and says, 'Monte, please, you hit a home run for me?' I told him, 'Jorge, damn, don't you see how hard that pitcher —it was Lazaro Salazar—is throwing?'

"Jorge keeps on urging, says he'll give me money. All I could do was smile at him and walk away.

"When I get back to the plate, Campy puts his mask up on his head and says, 'What was that about, man?' And I tell him to call for a good pitch for me—Jorge just offered me money if I could hit a homer off Salazar. Campy says, 'Not in this lifetime.'

"But I hit one over the center-field fence anyway! And we win. After I touched home plate, there's Jorge hugging me and slipping me $500.

"And there's Campy shaking his head. He says, 'You got to be the luckiest son of a bitch on the planet.' I laughed and said, 'C'mon, now,' and handed him half the money."

The old ballplayer folded his fingers behind his head with another big smile. "That's Monte," he said.

The boy was laughing. "For real?" he said.

And then fog wiped the scene away. The next replacement was a street-level view of a New York City neighborhood.

The boy had never seen so much traffic in his life. They were looking at the corner of Madison Avenue and East 45th

Street. A skyscraper was fronted by a bronze-colored overhang with the legend "Hotel Roosevelt."

It was December 3rd. Christmas was already alive in the city and the store windows looked like picture postcards. A fresh one-inch blanket of snow covered the sidewalk. The scene outside shifted past the Roosevelt Grill, where the early lunch crowd was arriving, to three black men inside a rising elevator.

"I'll be damned," the old ballplayer said. "What in the world is Paul Robeson doing there?"

"Man, there's a new force whistling in the wind here in 1943," Josh said. "The unions just held a big parade last month, marching for baseball integration in this town. Editors are writing editorials in the Amsterdam News, the Pittsburgh Courier, the Chicago Defender and other African-American newspapers.

"As you know well, Paul was Paul. He could do things others could not. He demanded and got a meeting with the major-league owners after he pressured the commissioner. The men with him in that elevator were William Patterson, who founded the Abraham Lincoln School of Research, and Ismael Flory, editor of a left-of-center black newspaper, The New World.

"Commissioner Landis had told Robeson to bring anyone he wanted with him. But when they reached the meeting room, the other two were ushered into another room nearby."

The old ballplayer and the boy watched in astonishment as Robeson, speaking to the group of team owners, who had been prepped by Landis, stood up to speak:

"The time has come when you must change your attitude toward Negroes," he began. "Because baseball is a national game, it is up to baseball to see that discrimination does not become an American pattern. And it should do so this year, because a thing like this—Negro ballplayers becoming a part of the great national pastime of America—could make a great difference in what people all over the world would feel toward us."

The owners sat stone-faced. When Robeson finished, they politely applauded in unison, almost as if on cue. Then Robeson opened the floor for questions. There were none—just dead, cold silence. Lip service, as always when the topic was baseball integration, had triumphed again.

"Disgusting," Josh Gibson interjected, "but not surprising. It's the same old crap. They never wanted us. They put Jackie Robinson and Larry Doby through hell four years later. Tried their best to chase 'em out. The pitchers threw at them, tried like hell to hit them. A lot of players, managers, and fans called them niggers.

"But the owners were right about one thing. They were right to ignore old Josh—Jet, you damn well know why. I wanted to play up there in the majors. You bet I did. But not badly enough to take that garbage. They knew me well enough not to ask. Some people say they broke my heart. But I damn well would have broken a few heads if I had to go through that to play a game that they all knew I always could play better than anyone they had."

Josh paused to let his words sink in.

Just before the fog rolled in to dissolve the scene away, the three watched Commissioner Landis leaving the hotel with the owner of the Red Sox, Tom Yawkey.

"The hell with those bastards," Josh said, quietly seething. "Yawkey will be the last major-league owner to let a brother set foot on his precious ball field—and that was 16 years away. And the commissioner would be dead a year after that meeting. He left this earth having made sure that no black man ever played a game in the so-called big leagues in his lifetime."

The fog returned.

Chapter 7
Max: An American Dream Denied

The boy, now totally schooled in the surreal routine, looked out the window and waited for the next adventure. He felt like a spectator at the greatest light show of all time, a kind of Fourth of July fireworks display, combined with a volcanic explosion. As the garish laser bolts streaked across the sky, they were interspersed with a cascade of free-falling symbols of geometric figures, punctuation marks, and what appeared to be depictions of busts of historic figures.

"Wow, Pop Pop," the boy asked. "What is going on out there?"

"Tell him this," the ghost said. "We got to travel back in time again, but this time to a place that was a far cry from Chicago or any other place we been so far on this trip. Tell him not many folks, even ghosts, ever go back there. Tell him we travelin' so far off the beaten track we sailin' through Father Time's wastebasket to a place that, as far as the lily-white major leagues was concerned, might as well have been in a foreign country.

"We goin' to Pleasantville, New Jersey, Jet. It ain't Chicago or even Newark. But in the spring of 1935, in the heart of the

Great Depression, it becomes the best place I know of to make this particular point to the boy. We're stopping by to see a future teammate of yours, a guy I used to hit against. But you might not recognize him. 'Cause in this incarnation, he's only 16 years old."

The first thing the boy saw after the lights and fog disappeared was a street sign that read "Ansley Blvd." Down the road, they could see Ansley Field, which sat behind the old red-brick Pleasantville High School and overlooked the bay. The unfenced little park was immediately identified as a baseball setting by the permanent backstop and the wooden bleachers that could sit up to 500.

"Where are we?" the boy asked the old ballplayer.

"Tell the boy we in 1935," Josh said. "We're five miles south of Atlantic City, 60 miles north of Philadelphia. And that"—he unleashed another booming peal of laughter—"basically puts us flat in the middle of nowhere."

"So why are we here?"

"We are here to show the boy the difference for us between 1935, where we are now, and 1963, where you and he are from. And we are here to make sure he understands that we had pioneers—hell, you and me were two of them—who kept the dream alive but who never got to live the end of that struggle. We are here to meet that six-foot-four-inch stringbean right-handed pitcher with the thick glasses over there, the guy throwing to his high school coach right now. Does he look a little familiar to you?"

The old ballplayer directed the boy's attention toward the skinny pitcher. "There is something about that young man that makes me feel I've seen him somewhere before," he said. "But I just can't recollect where."

The coach was pounding the pocket of his catcher's glove

and shouting encouragement toward his pitcher. Then the kid cut loose, and the sound of his fastball burying itself in the coach's mitt sounded like the crack of a Winchester rifle.

The old ballplayer had been staring hard at the tableau. He put an arm around the boy's shoulders and whispered, "Just look at the way he throws. Look how far he brings his arm back. Look at those spaces, the way he anchors his right leg behind him when he releases the ball and the way his left foot winds up when he finishes. You feel like you could drive a truck through that space. That powerful body movement is what generates the velocity. He could be throwin' an 85- or 90-mile-an-hour fastball, and he's still just a kid.

"And . . . well, damn, yeah, that's sure enough Max Manning. Long before he was my teammate on the Eagles. He got a little bigger and sure threw a hell of a lot faster over the next decade. Boy, I remember once when . . ."

"Jet, we ain't got time for any more old-timey memory-lane stuff," Josh told him. "We gonna show the boy the real thing."

Now a modest crowd had filed into the bleacher seats. Four men from the stands had moved down to the field and were in the coach's face. They were mad as hell.

Josh, the old ballplayer, and the boy could hear everything the men were yelling at the coach. His name was Emory Wilbur "Ty" Helfrich. Once upon a time he had played second base for the Brooklyn Tip Tops of the Federal League. That was in 1915; the Federal League was made up of major-leaguers who told the National and American League owners to go to hell because the salaries were so lousy, so they started a league of their own.

They could see he was still plenty tough. He didn't back up when one of the men stepped toward him. The man was so angry that spit was flying as he yelled.

"You got just one nigger on this team," he railed, "and it's only one, so we looked the other way! But we have sons on this team—and you ain't gonna pitch that nigger when one of our boys could be pitching."

"I coach this team!" Helfrich shouted back. "I'm as white as you are, and I don't give a damn if he's purple. He's my pitcher because he's the best one I got. You don't like it, don't stay. Now get the hell off my field!"

"Wow," the boy said. "When I grow up, I hope I get a coach like that."

"Tell him," Josh said to the old ballplayer, "when he gets older, that won't be a problem."

Just then, three white men in the fifth row got up and started to leave. One of them, a man named Max Bishop, was a scout for the Detroit Tigers. He had received a letter about this kid from Pleasantville who was striking everybody out; so he came to town to see for himself. He didn't know the young man was black. Now Bishop knew, and he was leaving.

"Did you really get to play with Mr. Manning on the Eagles?" the boy asked his grandfather.

"He was my teammate and my friend," the old ballplayer said. "And he was good. We called him Dr. Cyclops because of his thick glasses. If a rookie was leading off in the first inning, Max would throw his first pitch over the kid's head, and then our catcher would say, 'Best not dig in too close to the plate, 'cause he don't know where the ball is going and neither do I.' Then that kid would pull back from the plate just enough so that he was dead meat on three straight outside curveballs.

"Max never got to play in the white man's major leagues. But the year we won the Negro Leagues World Series, he went on a barnstorming tour with the Satchel Paige All-Stars and pitched against Bob Feller's Major League All-Stars. When they hit Dayton, Ohio, Max struck out 14 batters, including Charlie Keller, the great Yankee, three times. He joined us in 1938, and after each season he pitched in the winter leagues in Puerto Rico, Cuba, Mexico, Venezuela, the Dominican Republic. After he left the Eagles, he pitched a little in Canada in the Provincial League. He pitched just about everywhere except in the so-called major leagues of the U.S. of A."

Jet turned to the ghost. "I'm gonna tell the boy something you never knew. Listen and you'll learn something about how dirty they played Max."

"So he never played in what they called big-league baseball?" the boy asked.

"Well, almost. Jackie Robinson and Larry Doby crossed the color line into the majors in 1947. The following year, Max was warming up at Ruppert before a game and a fella we all knew named Alex Pompez leans over from a third-base box seat and tells him to come over. Alex was a Negro League player who once owned the New York Cubans, and that day he was a New York Giants scout.

"Here's what Max told me about that day:

'Alex said they'd been watching me and they liked what they saw. He asked me how I'd like to pitch for the New York Giants. He handed me a business card and told me to meet him at the Stadium Tavern around the corner after the game. So I went to meet him. Hell, what Eagle wouldn't have? Alex said I'd have to pitch for them in Jersey City a time or two and then they'd call me up because they needed pitchers badly. He said to be there on Thursday.

'Well, I had a contract with the Eagles. So I told him to call Mrs. Manley and straighten it out with her, and then nobody and nothin' in this world could keep me away from Jersey City on Thursday.

'Alex looked at me kinda funny and said, "Max, we ain't payin' that lady nothin'. You be there Thursday if you want to pitch for the Giants, or stay here pitchin' for that old lady for peanuts and her all-black customers. It's all the same to me."

'So I told him I wanted it more than he could ever know, but I had a contract and I couldn't just walk away. Alex just shook his head, threw some money on the table, and walked out without another word. If you don't have honor, what do you have?'

Jet paused. "That's the way Max was raised. Because of that, it's as close as he ever got to the major leagues."

The boy stared thoughtfully. "Would you have gone if you had a contract with Mrs. Manley?" he asked.

"Boy, I just don't know. We all wanted it so badly and we all knew we were good enough, so I just don't know. But I know this. If it happened, I wish I'd had his courage. Max was a rare man. When his arm went bad, he went over to Glassboro College and got his degree and taught sixth grade back at Pleasantville for twenty-eight years.

"I asked him once if he was bitter about what happened. And he showed me just how much character he had.

"He said, 'Jet, if I had gone to the majors, I never would have gone back to college. Never would have helped all those kids I taught. So I guess things just worked out the way they were supposed to work.'"

"Well," said Josh, "likewise, I know something you don't about Max! I'm gonna tell you now, then you can tell the boy while we're travelin' to our next stop. When Max was in the Army, he drove fuel supplies to General Patton's tanks through the bombs and the artillery shells during the Battle of the Bulge at Bastogne. No matter what those major-league owners thought, he was sure enough a real American.

"But back when he was drafted, 1942, they sent him to the

Richmond Army Air Base down in Virginia and assigned him to the 316th Aviation Squadron. That put him, like every other black man in the army, in an all-black unit commanded by a white officer.

"This white boy had a particular thing about Max. He didn't like the way he talked, the way he walked, the way he carried himself. He looked at Max as an uppity nigger with an attitude, lacking humility, and he treated him that way. He was a racist bully.

"Well, things weren't exactly great between the locals and the post, with all those black soldiers running around their Southern town. So somebody got the idea that the Army should put a baseball team together and invite town teams to come to the post to play them for the public-relations value. And this white boy was to be its manager.

"One day, he finds out Max was a bona fide professional pitcher in the Negro National League before he was drafted. He had no idea what cities had Negro National League teams, and he didn't give a damn. All he knew was that a pro pitcher, even a black one, was better than no pitcher.

"So he cozies up to him nice-like and tells him, 'Boy, you gonna be my ace pitcher.' And Max thinks about this guy and the way he treats the men in his command, and he says, 'I don't think so.'

"Now the guy gets furious. 'Boy, you ain't got a choice,' he says. 'I'm not asking you. I'm telling you. That's a direct order and you can't refuse.' And Max says, 'I don't think so.'

"And they throw him in the stockade for 15 days. When Max's fiancee hears about it back in New Jersey, she hops a bus and rides straight through to Richmond. When she gets to the base, they refuse to let her see him. And they sent her back home. Neither one of them ever forgot that.

"I don't know what happened to that arrogant son of a bitch

who did that to them. But I know Max Manning drove through all hell to get that fuel to General Patton's tanks, and neither Max nor Patton didn't care a damn whether the drivers were white or black.

"Now," Josh said, eyebrows raised, "you tell me which one was the real American: Max or that cracker."

Chapter 8
An Infield for the Ages

Suddenly, the three were standing at the players' entrance to Ruppert Stadium—back where the journey began.

"This is where we started, Pop Pop," the boy said to the old ballplayer. "Does that mean the trip is over?"

"I don't think so," he told his grandson. And in his heart, he knew it couldn't be.

"You damn well know it ain't, Jet," the ghost said, "and you tell him that. We back in 1939 here—because we got a chance to show the boy the greatest infield that never played in the major leagues. But they still were the greatest infield that ever played the game anywhere—and I mean anywhere—on this damn planet. You knew 'em. You even played with one of them."

Their view now was from the roof next to the press box behind home plate. Looking down, they saw a packed house, although it was more than an hour before game time and the Eagles infielders were still practicing. Nobody comes to a ball game that early just to watch infield practice. Batting practice? Maybe. But to watch guys warm up by making throws they could make 100 times with their eyes closed? Only here.

The infield grass across the river in Brooklyn and Manhattan and the Bronx was major-league. But it belonged to somebody else. Here in Newark, this was North Jersey's own infield. These were North Jersey's own infielders putting on their very own show.

Of all the pregame rituals in the history of the game America loves, this is the unchallenged most boring: four guys making 100 throws they could make every hour with their eyes closed.

But not here. Not these four.

Mule Suttles at first, Dick Seay at second, Willie Wells at short, Ray Dandridge at third. They called themselves the Million-Dollar Infield, although if you combined all their Negro League salaries, it might not top more than $650 a month.

"Wow!" the boy shouted. He had just seen Seay, the second baseman, dive to his right, make the pickup, whirl, and throw right on the money to first. "That's Dick Seay," the old ballplayer said. "He was an up-and-down hitter, from below .200 up to about .258—but he ain't out there because he can hit. He could be the slickest second baseman anywhere.

"That fella at first is Mule Suttles. He can play first and the outfield—and he hit more home runs than Josh Gibson."

Gibson shook his head so hard he almost dislodged it from his transparent shoulders. "Why you want to tell a lie like that? Musta been bad records. Who the hell kept statistics like that? Probably the damn bat boy."

"Like I said," the old ballplayer told the boy, enjoying the sight of Josh's anger, "Mule had power—so much so that every time he came to bat with men on base, the fans would chant, 'Kick, Mule, kick!' He swung a rare 50-ounce bat. One winter-league season down in Cuba, he hit a homer at Tropicana Park that cleared a 60-foot-high fence in center and landed in the ocean. He was so powerful that . . ."

"Enough with Mule's power!" Josh interrupted. "Why don't you tell him about Red Moore?"

The old ballplayer laughed. "Actually," he told the boy, "there was another first baseman back when they were called the Million-Dollar Infield. His name was Red Moore, and like the ballplayers say about great-fielding first basemen, he could really pick it. I wish I could have seen him."

And suddenly, he did. Infield practice down below was almost done. But the first baseman at the bag now was thinner and taller. He seemed to revel in his own motion.

Wells and Dandridge were smiling as they deliberately made low throws, forcing Red Moore to scoop them up in a long, sweeping motion accompanied by "oohs" and "ahhs" from the crowd. He got an ovation when he caught the last three throws behind his back.

Pregame was over. While they waited for the start of the game, the old ballplayer filled the boy in on the rest of the infield.

"Willie Wells was a shortstop for the ages," he said. "He played four positions and managed. Baseball was his life for twenty-five years—for teams in nine cities. He also played in Mexico, where they called him El Diablo, because opposing pitchers and baserunners swore he played the game like a devil. He even managed in Canada. He played in eight East-West All-Star games."

"Tell me about the third baseman, Pop Pop," the boy said. "He doesn't look much like an athlete. He's short and he's kinda stumpy. And from here he looks like he's kinda bowlegged."

"That's because he is—you picked that up, boy. He is the unlikeliest-looking athlete I ever saw. But don't get fooled. He was so bowlegged yet so quick laterally that when he played in

Cuba they said a train could get through that space between his knees but not a ground ball, ever. His old teammate Monte Irvin said that Ray considered he had a bad year if he made as many as four errors in a season.

"He had lightning reflexes. And from his first pro game, with the Detroit Wolves, he proved he had a skill that few ever had: If he saw a hitter swing just once, it was enough. It taught him where to play that guy to get an extra jump. It was like he had a filing cabinet in his head filled with data on every hitter he ever played against. He never forgot a man's tendencies."

"But, hey"—the old ballplayer pointed down to the field—" they're playing the Homestead Grays down there. We're in the fifth inning. And look who's coming to the plate. My dear old friend Mr. Josh Gibson. I believe Mr. Gibson is talking—or yelling?—toward Mr. Dandridge."

"Now hold it right there, Jet," Josh bristled. "The boy don't need to see nor hear this nonsense, and—"

"—too late, Josh! You shoulda thought of that sooner. It's your tour, but you musta forgot this part. So turn on that voodoo-hoodoo machine, or whatever it is, and let the boy hear."

"Damn! I did forget this part. Guess I got to oblige. . ."

The old ballplayer and the boy were tuned into the dialogue:

Dandridge: Hey, Josh, I'm right here, right where I know you gonna hit it. Think you can get it past me?

Gibson: Better duck, you runt. I'm gonna knock your head off with the first swing.

Dandridge: First you got to hit it, Josh, and on the off-chance you do, I'm gonna nail your big fat ass no matter where the ball goes.

Jet's smile broadened. He told the boy, "Ray got so far into Josh's head that he made one of the greatest hitters who ever lived ignore the first rule of great hitting: Hit the ball where it's pitched. Instead, Josh reached for an outside pitch and desperately tried to pull it instead of hitting it to the opposite field. His rage may have compounded the force of his swing. Dandridge went down to his knees to stop the bullet. He didn't even bother to get up. He yelled at Gibson, 'Run, Josh, run!' He held the ball until the last possible instant, then fired and nipped him at first by a half-step."

"That's enough!" Gibson hollered at the old ballplayer. "Just do what you're supposed to do. Tell him about Dandridge in Mexico."

Meanwhile, down on the field, Leon Day was in control. He gave up a scratch hit in the third and nothing else. As the Grays came to bat in the seventh, that scratch single was the only ball hit out of the infield.

The old ballplayer continued, "Well, there came a time with Dandridge, like with so many others in the league, that he had to go where he could make some money. Mrs. Manley wouldn't get up off another dollar for him. Then along came Jorge Pasquel. You remember him. He was the guy bringing black ballplayers to Mexico and later the white boys from the major leagues. He made Dandridge an offer. Ray gave Manley a chance to match it, but she didn't offer anything. Ray packed up and went to Mexico."

"What about the language?" the boy asked. "Don't Mexican players speak Spanish?"

"Yes, Jeffy—good. But we know what baseball's white power structure never understood. We knew most of us was just as bright as the folks who didn't think we were. Whether we went to Mexico or Cuba or Puerto Rico or Venezuela, most of us picked up Spanish more and more the longer we played.

"We also picked up friends down there. Leon and Willie went with us, and even Josh joined us on the Veracruz team.

And Ray, well, he played longer in Mexico than any other guy from our league. A couple of times he came back to Newark, and each time Pasquel gave him more money, and each time Mrs. Manley said, 'I'm not gonna overpay you.' So he kept going back to Mexico.

"Then Pasquel raided the majors and the white boys started to come. And Dandridge got to make the same money as Pasquel's newly welcomed major-leaguers. He was earning $10,000 a year and had a free house and a maid.

"You ought to tell him," the ghost interrupted, "that Dandridge hit .355 lifetime in the Negro Leagues, .347 in exhibition games played against white major-leaguers in his career, and about the same in Mexico. He also had a thirty-two-game hitting streak, a record, and managed a team to the Mexican League championship."

"Well, I was really fixin' to tell him about Dandridge and the Mexican army!" He turned back to the boy. "Lots of folks don't know how much he dominated the league and how just about all of Mexico loved him. They used to call him Mamerto.

"In some Latino places, that word means stupid. In others, forgetful. But in Mexico it meant 'man endowed with super-fantastic physical gifts.' No baseball player in Mexico or anywhere else had the ability to do the things you were sure nobody could do—until Ray did them.

"So one day he gets in an argument with Jorge Pasquel. People who want to keep walkin' around didn't dare do that. The argument was over money. Ray says, "I quit—this time for good. I'm taking a train to Texas.

"He gets on a train. About 10 minutes after it departs, it suddenly stops. All these soldiers with guns are walking up and down the aisle yelling, 'Ray Dandridge, raise your hand!'

"Ray puts a newspaper in front of his face and kinda ducks

down. But a soldier says, 'You are Ray Dandridge—you come with us.'

"So now he's back in Pasquel's office—this is one of the most powerful guys in the country. Pasquel is staring at him, and then he laughs and says, 'You win!' He gave him $10,000 in cash. So Ray went back and played his ass off. Ray later used that money to buy his house in Newark."

The old ballplayer shook his head. "Pasquel . . . wow. He collected about twenty-three major-leaguers. One of them was Sal Maglie, who learned different curveballs based on the high altitudes in Mexico. When he returned to the Giants, he became a Hall of Fame pitcher.

"Maglie had never seen a Negro League game," he added, "and knew nothing of its superstars. But he never saw anyone play third base like Ray. One day he asked him where he came from, and Ray laughed and said, 'Same country as you, boy.'"

Even Josh laughed at the anecdote. "Sounds just like him," he said. "You know what he said when they inducted him in the Hall of Fame? He was in his seventies by then and he told them, 'Thanks for letting me smell the roses, but what took you so long?'"

Their laughter was interrupted by a commotion. The crowd was roaring as a rally by the Grays gained momentum. All the infielders were clustered around Day, looking toward the dugout. The manager, Dick Lundy, emerged and headed out to join them.

"Yeah, that's Lundy," the old ballplayer said. "He was the shortstop before Wells came. In those days they called him the King. He taught Dandridge and Wells a lot."

He didn't take the ball from Day. Instead he huddled with all of them. "I think he's telling Leon to keep it low, to force a ground ball off this hitter," Jet said. From their vantage point they read the big scoreboard next to the Wolf's Head Oil sign in right field. The bases were loaded with nobody out and the Eagles ahead, 2-0.

Then, in a single sequence, the boy finally understood why they were called the Million-Dollar Infield. Before the three rooftop spectators realized it, the batter had squared to bunt. He didn't get the ball down. Instead it was a soft, very low blooper that traveled maybe twenty feet.

It should have hit the dirt of the baseline, but Dandridge stretched his body like it was an uncoiled spring. His glove scraped the ground as he caught it. Wells was covering third and took the throw Dandridge made from his back; Wells tagged the runner off third and then fired to Seay, who was covering first as that runner desperately tried to scramble back.

"Triple play! Triple play!" the boy shouted. He jumped so hard the old ballplayer had to keep him from falling off the roof.

"That's all he needed to see—we're done here," Josh told the old ballplayer. "Just make sure you remind him that not one of these guys ever got to play a single minute of major-league baseball all of their lives."

He grimaced. "But what he'll see next makes me even madder every time I think about it."

Chapter 9
The Promises of Liars

They had no idea where they were going. But they had long since put their itinerary in the hands of the late Josh Gibson and the barrage of fog that he could conjure up—as well as whatever unseen forces were providing the long-gone venues that appeared in their wake and were steering the old Eagles bus along its mystical way.

The boy was asleep with his head on the old ballplayer's shoulder, and Josh was staring at Jefferson in a way that was part puzzled and part anticipation.

"You never asked me," the ghostly catcher told the old ballplayer.

"Asked you what?"

"Asked me why you, and why this boy. Why have I attached myself to the two of you? There are other Negro League players still alive and I'm sure they have grandsons. Have you wondered about that?"

"Look," the old ballplayer replied, "I don't know what I can or can't wonder about. First you break my leg. Then you come back as a ghost and scare me. And now . . . you expect me to believe I really have a nickel in this quarter! Josh, you might be the greatest hitter who ever lived, but you are an even greater pain in the ass."

There was silence inside the bus. Then Josh shattered it with his booming laugh.

"Jet," he said, through chuckling, "I always liked you. I respected you. You never knew it, but you were a hell of a problem for me each time I had to try to nail you when you were running to steal a base. I always admired you because I think you were probably the smartest and most articulate of our guys. And I always owed you because . . ."—Josh fixed his eyes on Jet's—"because, damn it, I broke your leg. I never told you when I was alive, Jet, but each time you bolted for second base and I came out of that crouch firing the ball, I believed, in my heart of hearts, it was the best against the best."

"I had no idea you felt that way," the old ballplayer said. "I thank you for telling me."

"Tell me this," Josh said. "You ever wonder why at first there were three of us visiting you: me, Satch, and Leon? It was because we hatched the idea among us. Where we come from now . . . you get to thinkin' a lot. You sit around talkin' about how good we were, and how good and bad at the same time our lives were.

"And then, I guess, it was Satch who said: 'Look at us . . . three old farts and our memories—and the game of baseball has it so good now that hardly anybody, even the young black players, remembers who we were. We left footprints, boys. Who will even remember to look for them?'

"Then it was Leon," Josh went on, "who played for a spell with you and who reminded that Baltimore reporter when Leon was on his deathbed that we were major-leaguers—all of us. And he said that maybe we need a messenger . . . a kind of Chief in Charge of Reminding.

"So here we are." Josh leaned forward in his seat to get a

better view of Jeffy's sleeping face on Jet's shoulder. "We could say you're the custodian of the messenger we need: the boy. He'll be the one that will tell the others who come after us. He will keep us alive in the minds of baseball fans who, without him, wouldn't even know we or our leagues, for that matter, even existed.

"Well, I said it. So . . . now we ain't got much time. We can't even stop here, so we got to do this part fast." He shifted in the other direction and pointed. "Look outside, tell me what you see. Because later when the boy wakes up, you got to tell him."

The old ballplayer peered through a milky-white haze. As it cleared, he was looking down at a street scene in Washington, D.C., sometime in the late 1930s. Both sides of the road were packed with cheering people.

The Washington Senators were marching through the streets to Griffith Stadium dressed in their home uniforms, as they traditionally did on Opening Day.

"Now," Josh instructed, "focus on that 79-year-old black man on your right. He's standing next to his grown son. It's just a few blocks from the house they live in with their families, at 13th and U Street. The old man"—Jet saw he was proudly holding a sign that said "I Saw Walter Johnson Pitch"—"and his son have been standing there for hours, waiting to see the team they both love. Now watch what happens."

Just as one of the players passed within a few feet, he glared at the old man, shouted something, stopped—and spit squarely in his face.

Josh and Jet stared in horrified silence. "Years later," the ghost finally said, "that son would say, 'My father never watched another baseball game from that day on.'"

Josh studied his friend's face. "You don't recognize the son," the ghost said. "You must be gettin' old, Jet. That's Sam Lacy."

Astonished, the old ballplayer nodded. "Right. It was him

and two other black sportswriters, Wendell Smith and Joe Bostic, who were the black standard-bearers who fought the hardest to break baseball's color barrier. Them, and a white Jewish Boston City Councilman everybody forgot, Isadore Muchnick. Sure, there was Branch Rickey, who signed Jackie Robinson, and Bill Veeck, who signed Larry Doby. But it was those black men who pushed baseball to get off its collective ass.

"Now," the ghost said, "we gonna make one last pass at D.C. You listen close to what happens. It was a meeting in 1936 between Lacy and Clark Griffith, who owned the Washington Senators. You knew Lacy, and so did I. If there is one thing nobody can challenge, it's that here was a guy who had no fear when it came to standing up for right against wrong.

"Old Clark Griffith," Josh continued, "he knew Lacy because as a kid, Lacy hung around the ballpark and ran errands for the players. Like the other owners Griffith didn't want a black man on his team, but unlike them, he gave Lacy a face-to-face hearing about it.

"The Homestead Grays had moved from Pittsburgh to Washington—you may remember I spent some time with them, hitting balls over your head at Griffith Stadium when your Eagles came to town."

"One ball," the old ballplayer retorted. "It was one ball, and if you recall I twisted my ankle or I would have caught it."

"You got your story," the ghost said, "and I got mine. Anyway, you can see right into that stadium office. Listen to this conversation."

Griffith: "I don't think it's a good idea, Sam. There are a lot of ballplayers from the South in our league. There'd only be trouble and confrontations."

Lacy: "Well, Mr. Griffith, think about the black players you have seen each time the Grays rented your stadium. You could end that national cliché about the Senators being first in war, first in peace, and last in the American League."

Griffith: "Like I said, Sam, just too many problems. And if we all did that, we'd put about four hundred black baseball players out of work."

Lacy: "Mr. Griffith, if I recollect correctly, when President Lincoln signed the Emancipation Proclamation, he put about four hundred thousand black folks out of work."

"Griffith isn't going to budge," Josh said as the tableau faded. "He proved that just after World War II ended. His all-star first baseman Mickey Vernon wrote him from where he was stationed in the South Pacific and said he'd been playing with a black who could hit with real power, field, and run. He added, 'We could use him.'

"Griffith wrote back, 'You think about playing first base and I'll think about who I want to sign.' The player was a guy we both knew. His name was Larry Doby.

"But I got to pass something else along for you to tell the boy. In 1942, the *Daily Worker*, a national communist paper that was read by a lot of people, forced the White Sox to give a tryout at their spring training camp in Pasadena to a guy who had excelled in four sports at UCLA. They did not sign him. His name was Jackie Robinson.

"The following month, our sportswriter friend Joe Bostic gorilla'ed his way into the Dodger camp at Bear Mountain, New York, and demanded tryouts for two black players, an Eagles pitcher named Terris McDuffie and Showboat Thompson, the first baseman with the New York Cubans. Rickey, who was looking to sign a black player at his own time of choosing, was furious with Bostic for doing that in front of the writers assigned to cover the Dodgers. Bostic was a New York celebrity, and he and Rickey would see each other often at Ebbets Field after Jackie became a Dodger, but Bostic and Rickey never spoke to each other again.

"Just filling you in, Jet," the ghost finished with a smile. "Now hang on—we about to make our real stop. Wake the boy up."

Peering through the fog, Josh and Jet could surmise from the clothes and the other cars that they were probably in 1945. When they passed by an old ballpark—with the left-field wall they call the Green Monster—he knew exactly where he was. He had never played in Fenway Park. But to him, anyone who didn't know about it must have been a volleyball player, because they sure as hell weren't connected to baseball.

They drove on for some time along busy Blue Hill Avenue, passed the Boston Zoo, and soon were in a section of town called Mattapan. The stores that bore family names in the window were clearly owned by Jews; 99 percent of Mattapan's residents were Jewish.

"What are we doing here?" the old ballplayer asked the ghost. "What's it got to do with us? I don't see one black face."

"You probably won't, Jet," Josh said. "But look over there. See that little storefront? That's the neighborhood office of Isadore Muchnick. He represents this part of town on the Boston City Council. He is a Harvard Law School grad. And he is going to embarrass the baseball power structure as it has never before been embarrassed. The issue"—he raised his eyebrows with a wicked smile—"is the guys in our league who could have played in theirs."

"But why here?"

"The man is on the telephone," the ghost said, "and he is talking to the general manager of the Boston Red Sox—a former player named Eddie Collins. For the first time in his life, Mr. Collins is going to have to think about guys like you and me, whether he likes it or not. So here we are in the man's place of business."

"You going to use that voodoo-hoodoo thing of yours so we can listen in?" Jet asked, grinning.

"It's already turned on. Tell the boy to pay attention."

Isadore Muchnick was leaning back in his swivel chair. A newspaper clipping was on the desk before him.

His voice rang out as he spoke on the phone. "You know my position about tying your team's refusal to try out black players to my objection to a blue-law waiver for you and the Red Sox. And my position is still the same. You know as well as do I that the Boston blue laws prohibit baseball on Sundays. And you always get a waiver, because those are big paydays for baseball.

"Well, you have ignored my proposal for a year. People are listening to me. I told you I will fight that waiver unless you start giving Negro players a chance. You scheduled one for April 12th for three ballplayers Wendell Smith agreed to bring. They're here in a hotel, and they're waiting. Now I want to read something to you that Wendell Smith wrote today."

Muchnick rolled his chair forcefully to his desk and grabbed the newspaper clipping. "'This is Boston, cradle of America's democracy,'" he read, his enunciation emphatic. "'I have three of Crispus Attucks' descendants with me. They are Jackie Robinson, Sammy Jethroe, and Marvin Williams. All three are baseball players, and they want to play in the major leagues . . . We have been here nearly a week now, but all our appeals for fair consideration and opportunity have been in vain.'"

"You broke our agreement!" Collins responded heatedly. "You weren't supposed to tell the press. That Smith piece was an embarrassment, but this morning Dave Egan of the Daily Record wrote that I am living in 1865 with my attitude, and I act like I live in Mobile, not Boston."

"Well," Muchnick said, "today's the 15th. You open the season on the 17th. You are not gonna stall past tomorrow, if that's your plan. I will introduce action against the waiver." He slammed the phone down.

At 10:30 the next morning, Muchnick and Smith led Williams, Jethroe, and Robinson to a side gate, where they were met by Sox scout Larry Woodall and coach Hugh Duffy. The Red Sox needed the help because the war had hit their roster hard. A small group of white players were working out, but they were ordered off the field. Robinson went to shortstop. Williams played second base. Sam Jethroe jogged to the outfield.

Smith and Muchnick sat watching in the stands, as did Red Sox manager Joe Cronin, who clearly was no fan of baseball integration. Nowhere to be seen were Collins and team owner Tom Yawkey.

"Hell, Jet, you and I know these guys well enough to be character witnesses," the ghost said. The boy—excited to be in yet another big-league park—clapped as Robinson and Williams fielded ground balls and practiced double plays, and gazed at Jethroe as he loped across the outfield to catch fly balls. Then the three took batting practice, with Robinson looking the most effective.

After an hour, they were handed forms to fill out. They left.

"They never heard from the Red Sox again," the old ballplayer muttered dejectedly, to the boy and the ghost as much as himself.

"But," he added after a pause, "Jethroe and Robinson eventually played, for the Boston Braves and the Dodgers. The Red Sox, though, let two major-leaguers slip away. That didn't surprise me."

"Why was that?" the boy asked.

"Because, my boy, the color line was broken by Jackie and

Larry Doby in 1947—but the Red Sox didn't sign a single black player until 12 years later. They were the last team in baseball to sign a black player. His name was Pumpsie Green." He gazed into the distance. "No wonder they went twenty years from the day Jackie and Larry broke through until the day they finally won a pennant."

"I'm glad you made that clear to him," Josh said. "But there's one more step in explaining how hard the struggle was. And we've still got a lot of ground to cover after that."

Chapter 10
To Live and Die in the Minors

Once again, the boy was asleep. That gave Josh the time he needed to explain what the next stop was all about.

"We are going to 1950," the ghost told the old ballplayer. "They finally broke the color line three years earlier, first with Jackie and then with Larry, but it's important that the boy knows that some of us who would surely have been major-league All-Stars still wound up forever on the outside looking in. Their last excuse was that they kept us out because it became a question of age—but it was them who sentenced us to grow older every year they had kept on Jim Crowing us.

"I guess," Jet interjected, "that means we're going back to pay another visit to Ray Dandridge. We both know what they did to him was a shame and a scandal. He could have kept playing at forty or forty-five. Hell, Biz Mackey was my playing manager when he was fifty-one, and he was a catcher. Who else but Dandridge is better to prove the point? I heard in his last year in baseball, he was the player-manager of the Bismarck Barons out in North Dakota. He hit .369—and he was forty-three years old."

Outside their windows, the fog began to build again. When it cleared, the view was of a business district in a big city.

The boy had awakened by then. "Why do all these buildings have American flags on them?" he asked the old ballplayer.

"Tell him," Josh said, "it's because today is the Fourth of July and in this town that means baseball—baseball here in the morning, baseball on the other side of the river in the afternoon. Seems like it's always been that way in these two towns."

The "two towns" were the Twin Cities of Minneapolis and St. Paul, two urban centers about nine miles apart that competed ferociously for industry and prestige. When Minneapolis declared itself the first city in the West, St. Paul retaliated by billing itself as the last city in the East. There was even a brief period in the mid-1960s where the two could not agree on a common calendar for Daylight Savings Time. As a result, there was a brief period when, incredibly, people commuting from Minneapolis arrived at work in St. Paul "an hour before they left."

But there were two things the Twin Cities indisputably shared: the Mississippi River and a fiery will to win the American Association baseball championship.

"They surely did dislike each other," the old ballplayer told the boy. "In 1923, there was a local baseball fight that took 12 cops to quiet down. There's a story that when the Irish in St. Paul wanted to celebrate St. Patrick's Day, they painted a green line down the middle of one of the bridges linking the two cities. But the city fathers on the Minneapolis side made them stop at the city limits."

The boy was gazing at some strange architecture just outside the window. The high, broad exterior and the beveled roof of the building's entrance looked very much out of place—like the entrance to a giant gingerbread house. After a few minutes, he was able to deduce it was a baseball park.

"Tell him that's Nicollet Park," the ghost said. "It was home field of the Minneapolis Millers. And since it's July 4th, we're going to a morning game. As soon as it's over, they'll get back on street cars and go over to Lexington Park in St. Paul to play the second game. The two things these two sets of fans have in common is dislike for each other and total love of baseball."

The ghost made mysterious gestures with his hands—a spin of his wrists, circular motions with his fingers—and suddenly the three of them were inside the park. It was the seventh inning. To their continued surprise, the first thing they saw was another player hustling into the home dugout to join the team. He had apparently been picked up at the train station by the team general manager an hour earlier and rushed over to Nicollet Park.

He was the only black man in either dugout.

"That looks like Mr. Dandridge," the boy said.

"It is," the old ballplayer replied. "And you are seeing history again. He's the first man of color to wear a Minneapolis uniform. If he gets in the game, he will be the first black man to play in this town."

The pitcher was a future major-leaguer named Mickey McDermott, who had already struck out 18 batters. The Millers were frustrated, going nowhere fast. The manager, Tommy Heath, looked toward the corner of the dugout and saw Dandridge. "This guy is killing us," Heath said. "You think you could get a hit off him?"

"That's what I'm here for," said Dandridge. He grabbed a bat.

"Watch this, boy," the old ballplayer said. "There are two ways to understand what's about to happen."

McDermott threw a fastball close enough to Dandridge's head to put him in the dirt. He got up and hit the next pitch— over the pitcher's head—into center field for a single.

"That," the ghost said to the old ballplayer, "was the answer so many of us could have given." He shook his head. "We weren't black men who played baseball. We were baseball men who happened to be black.

"You can also tell the boy this about Ray," Josh added. "Tell him that in this season, Dandridge will win the batting title with an average of .362. He'll lead the league's third baseman in fielding. And because he's so talented, the fans for the next three years will totally forget his skin color. To them, he isn't a black man. He's a Minneapolis Miller.

"The following year, he hit .311, won the MVP award, and the Millers won the pennant. He is thirty-seven years old. The color line had been modestly crossed for three years with a handful of black players in the majors. The New York Giants owned the Minneapolis franchise. At that moment they were in third place, behind the Dodgers and the Phillies. They were weak at third. Dandridge assumed they'd know what they had waiting in Minneapolis to come fill that hole. He was already the property of the Giants.

The boy turned his head back to the window. "So where are we going next?"

"I have a good guess," the old ballplayer replied. "The Polo Grounds—just across the Harlem River from Yankee Stadium. I think it's time you know about a less obvious but not less evil side of racism."

Out of the fog came a view of the interior of a New York City subway car. It rumbled its way into the 155th Street Station and shivered to a stop. Doors opened. The old ballplayer, the boy, and the ghost exited and climbed grimy stairs. The old ballpark loomed above them.

"You are going right into the Giants' center-field clubhouse," the ghost told the old ballplayer. "You're going to hear a shameless confession about racism three years after baseball told the world it had finally found its way into the 20th century. You remember Hank Thompson? Played infield and outfield with the Monarchs, had a brief fling with the St. Louis Browns. Eventually wound up with the Giants. He was better in the outfield, but they played him at third base because they had no options.

"Both Jack Lohrke and Bill Rigney were better at second and short, but they were moved over so Thompson could remain in the outfield, where he could contribute more. But they weren't natural third basemen. Thompson went back to third.

"So here we are. We're going to listen to a conversation where Thompson and Monte Irvin, the first black man to play for the Giants, still think they can win the 1950 National League pennant:

Thompson: "I don't belong at third. They can get more out of me in the outfield."

Irvin: "You know we're only six behind the Phillies and the Dodgers. It's only August. We could still win this thing. Makes sense if we can find a third baseman who can field and hit and improve us enough."

Thompson and Irvin [simultaneously]: "Ray Dandridge."

Thompson: "Why not?"

Irvin: "We got to talk to Leo [Durocher]."

Manager Durocher: "There's nothing I can do. Do you think I don't know all about him? Do you think I don't know what he's doing down there in Triple-A? Don't you think I spent a lot of time trying to make that case? I'd love to have him. You go to Chub [Feeney, the general manager]. He's the only one who can talk to the Man [Horace Stoneham, the owner], but this decision is far over my head. You can tell Chub I support your suggestion completely."

And the room seemed to spin and go dark. Then it was illuminated again, and the new view put them in the room with Irvin, Thompson, and Feeney.

"Move Hank back to the outfield, where he really helps? What do you think?" Feeney asked.

With a grin, Thompson said, "There is no better third baseman on this earth than Ray Dandridge. And he is a real hitter."

"It makes sense," Feeney said. "I could talk to Horace. It could work. But there are two of you guys on this roster. Which of you would be willing to go back to the minors?"

Here the old ballplayer could barely control himself. "Boy," he said with quiet fury, "don't ever forget that conversation you just heard. What it means is that for all the talk about ending the color ban . . . for all the time they spend patting themselves on the back about being sooo American . . . taking bows because they say they had become sooo color-blind . . . the truth was— well, let me put it this way so you will never forget.

"Jackie Robinson and Larry Doby were supposed to have shattered major-league baseball's color line forever, just three years before you heard this garbage. But Ray Dandridge, who had been a professional ballplayer for 19 years . . . Ray Dandridge, who had once been part of black baseball's Million-Dollar Infield, in name, things being what they were, not salary . . . Ray Dandridge, who was a national hero in Mexico and Cuba and Puerto Rico before the Giants were caught up in this decision—Ray Dandridge was doomed to permanent exile. You heard it. The sons of bitches admitted they had a lousy unspoken quota rule they would rather keep than have a chance to win the National League pennant.

"Remember exactly the way I said it, boy. Nobody had the guts to look Irvin or Thompson or Dandridge in the eye and admit it."

The ghost of Josh Gibson gazed eye-to-eye at the old

ballplayer. "Damn," he muttered. "I'm proud of you, Jet. That's exactly what I wanted the boy to know. The Giants didn't take Dandridge to camp the next season. He went back to Minneapolis and won the MVP and a Gold Glove. But the Giants forgot him. A year later, in the same town, he hit .324. The Giants said he was too old to consider.

"Larry Doby once told me, 'When you mention Brooks Robinson or Billy Cox, you're talking about great-fielding third basemen. Ray Dandridge was better, or at least as good. And he wasn't just a .280 hitter. One or two guys might be able to field with him. But the way he hit for average, he'd leave them in the dust.'

"Doby was right. Now I'll tell you something you didn't know. Years after Ray played his last game, Stoneham held a reunion, and somehow Dandridge got invited. 'I'm sorry,' Stoneham said, 'but you meant so much to those fans, and to the Millers' gate receipts, that I just couldn't bring you up.' Right—like any major-league owner gave a crap about the fans in his minor-league franchises.

"But Ray had his say," Josh went on with a sardonic grin. "He looked at Stoneham for a minute, and then he said, 'Mr. Stoneham, all I ever wanted was just to play one game in a major-league uniform. To step into the batter's box one time. To play one inning in the field. That would have made it all worthwhile for me.

"'I can't forgive you.'

"Stoneham reached into his pocket and handed Ray $1,000. Guilt money, that's all it was. Do you think that's a fair price tag on the career he and the Giants stole?"

The old ballplayer repeated every word to the boy. Then he added, "Years from now, when you tell this story, Jeffy, never forget to add that he died as the best third baseman in the world never to play in major-league baseball."

Chapter 11
Into the Belly of the Beast

T he old ballplayer and the boy had absolutely no idea what they might see next. Jet told himself that maybe Jackie and Larry were next. And that he looked forward to. He had played with both, and Robinson, of course, was the major force in the pantheon of those who led the march to baseball equality.

"I'm guessing," the old ballplayer told the boy, "that with all you've learned, it's now time to see the way they broke the color line and how the struggle didn't exactly end there."

"You are right!" Josh said. "We have a long way to go on this journey."

He shifted in his seat. "I'm sure you already told him how Branch Rickey had his 'hammers of hell' session with Jack—about what people would try to do to him and how he had to turn the other cheek. Damn, he had to turn it so often his head might as well have been on a damn swivel."

The old ballplayer chimed in. "They threw pitches at him. They spiked him. They cursed at him. And the fans were even worse in most places. Jackie wasn't our best player, but he was the one who took the crap and earned respect and paved the way. He was spectacular."

"I can't argue against that," Josh interjected, "but I still don't like the way he talked about the Negro Leagues." He paused. "We had a lot better than him. Satchel Paige and Monte Irvin and Roy Campanella and, well, me. And if you went back even further, there were older guys who were far better.

"You know, Jet, we all wanted him to make it. But we all were afraid he wouldn't and that would be the end of the chance for all of us. So we did try to help him.

"We all needed somebody to make it," the ghost added. "The word was that Robinson appeared to have the inside track, so we all tried to make him a little better. We knew if the first guy failed, that would be the end for us."

Jet nodded. His expression clearly showed how happy he was that their reminiscences had landed on the topic of Robinson. "He sure wasn't no shortstop, although he insisted he was," the old ballplayer said. "I know it was Willie Wells who showed him how to make the double-play pivot when the Dodgers made him a second baseman.

"We all knew that he was not the best we had, because of his inexperience," the old ballplayer told the boy. "And it's certainly true that the stolen bases belonged to Robinson's natural talent. So did the consistent bat, the diving catches. But, yes, the double-play pivot that finally gave him a major-league position, that came from Willie."

"Even on the Eagles," the old ballplayer said, "we knew he really wasn't a shortstop. The story I heard was that the Monarchs were playing against your Grays, and Cool Papa Bell was finishing his career with that team. They say he was still the fastest guy ever in our league—nobody could motor like Cool Papa.

"A couple of the Monarchs talked to Cool Papa about it before the game. I heard Cool Papa twice made Jackie go into the hole, not his best move as a shortstop, and beat his arm for two infield hits. We also heard that he stole four bases that day —and each time he beat Jackie's tag, he got up, brushed off the dirt, and told him, 'They got dozens of white guys up in the majors who can make that same slide every day, so you better pay attention, son.'"

"Well, I never heard that story," the ghost said, "but it sounds right to me. I mean, Jackie sure didn't think much of our league. Probably they had a little more money and were a little better organized back at UCLA. But in the end, with all that competitive fire in him, he was a fantastic player.

"I'll admit that he damn sure learned fast as a big-leaguer. I think he was chosen because he came from a big city, which most of us didn't, and he had played with white boys in college. I guess Branch Rickey thought that would help."

"Well," the old ballplayer said, "he made it in a way that they will remember forever. Maybe he was in too much of a hurry to think back on our league much. That's all right with me—that made a guy like Bill Veeck look at our league and he ended up getting Doby. The fact is that Jackie deserves our admiration because he was first and if he had failed there would have been no second.

"Because of Jackie," he added, "we never had to look back again. That includes the young ones who came after us. You could argue he should not have been the first. But he was. Because of him, there was no looking back."

The boy came awake just then.

"At his age," his grandfather said, "I don't think he needs to hear the way this conversation has been going. I think right now he needs only to know how Jackie prevailed when the world thought he couldn't."

Another look out the window. "So where are we going?"

"We're there, Jet," said Josh. "Look through the fog—see all those signs in French? We in Montreal. We're arriving at Delorimier Stadium. The Montreal Royals were the Dodger farm team where Rickey sent Jackie. This was where Jackie was under the microscope. This was where the so-called experiment began."

As they focused on the interior of the stadium, there was a tremendous amount of noise and excitement: The scoreboard showed the game had just ended, and the Montreal Royals had won the International League championship.

"So why is Mr. Robinson running away from all those white people?" the boy asked.

"Best way to answer that, Jet, is for us to change the scene," the ghost said.

And it did again. "This is the conference room at Ebbets Field," Josh went on as the picture materialized. "Here's where the decision was made about where to send Jackie Robinson to play a minor-league season. That guy"—he pointed—is named Clay Hopper. He became the manager of the Royals. You're gonna hear what he said back then. And then you'll hear what he said after Jackie drove his team to the International League title.

Hopper in the spring of 1946: "Do you really think a nigger is a human being, Mr. Rickey?"

Hopper in late 1946: "Robinson is a player who must go to the majors. He's a big-league ballplayer, a good team hustler, and a real gentleman."

The boy looked at the old ballplayer. "OK," he said. "But I still want to know why all those white people are chasing Mr. Robinson across the field."

The old ball player smiled broadly. "As I recall from my playing days," he answered, "there was a fella named Sam Maltin, who wrote for the Pittsburgh Courier. He and Wendell Smith and

Sam Lacey were the three black writers who were there. What you're seeing is the day the Montreal Royals won it all. Maltin hit it right on the head when he watched the crowd mob Jackie—he wrote, 'It was probably the only day in history that a black man ran from a white mob with love instead of lynching on its mind.'

The scene outside the window dissolved as though it were a television picture, "and now it's morphing into the very next year," Josh began. "The Dodgers . . . well, hell, take a closer look. You're going to see a Dodgers preseason game at Cincinnati. But before the boy sees it, Jet, do you remember the revolt in the Dodger clubhouse?"

"Damn right I do," Jet said with heat, "and so would anyone else who played in our league. What was happening, Jeffy"—he turned back to the boy—"was a small revolution in the Brooklyn clubhouse. It wasn't pretty. Probably the most popular Brooklyn player was an outfielder named Dixie Walker. He spoke up for a few others who planned to refuse to play on a team with a black man.

"People in Brooklyn were saying Branch Rickey was up against the wall on this, because the last thing Dodger fans would stand for was for Rickey to bench or trade Dixie—his nickname among fans, in colloquial Brooklynese, was 'the people's cherce.'

"Rickey solved that in a hurry. He traded him, all right—to the Pittsburgh Pirates, who'd finish seventh in the eight-team National League. That ended that revolution. But Rickey had a lot of help from an unexpected source."

"What's that water down there?" the boy interrupted as he pointed.

"That's the Ohio River!" the ghost shouted. "Tell him to take a good look at that little ballpark, because the Cincinnati Reds left it a long time ago. It was called Crosley Field, and it was the first major league ballpark to have lights for night baseball."

"I believe we're here to see Jackie's first trip to a Southern National League park, " the old ballplayer told the boy. "Cincinnati and St. Louis were solid Jim Crow towns. For a long time after we broke the color line, black players couldn't even stay at the hotels or eat at most of the restaurants."

Robinson was playing first base then, and the Dodgers were taking infield practice. The boy could see a huge crowd had congregated on the first base side of the stands. They were chanting and jeering and threatening—"Nigger, go back to the cotton field!" and "Snowflake!" and "Shoeshine boy!"—and they were joined by Cincinnati players yelling from their dugout.

"These people are horrible," the boy said.

"Never mind them," Josh said. "Tell him to look over yonder."

A Dodger player was walking slowly toward Jackie. "That's Pee Wee Reese, the captain and shortstop," the old ballplayer told the boy. "He grew up in racially segregated Louisville, right across the river. Obviously, he is white. Now watch what he does."

Reese paid no attention to the idiots in the stands or the cowards in the Reds' dugout. He calmly slipped an arm over Robinson's shoulder and started laughing like the two were sharing a big joke. "All the while," Jet said, "he acted like they couldn't even hear the idiots cursing and yelling. The more they laughed, the madder the idiots got.

"Years later," the old ballplayer said, "Jackie told Roger Kahn, the sportswriter from the New York *Herald Tribune*, that he never felt alone on a ball field again after that. The slurs took a few years to stop, but starting then Jackie knew he had team-mates to rely on."

"Yeah," Josh interjected, "but it sure as hell wasn't that simple. A month later, Stanley Woodward, the sports editor of the *Herald Tribune*, received a tip that the St. Louis Cardinals were planning to strike on their next visit to Ebbets Field if the Dodgers played Jackie.

"Stanley was the toughest guy ever to become a sports editor this side of Wyatt Earp. He had bad eyes and played college football at Amherst wearing glasses and a softball catcher's mask. When somebody remarked that a player who hit it could hurt himself, Stanly just smiled and said, 'Yeah, couldn't he?' In college he took Latin and Greek, and he was the only sports editor who could read *The Iliad* in its original language.

"Make sure you repeat this to the boy word for word," the ghost added, "because I want him to know that there was a very tough white guy who stepped up and struck a blow for our side when it counted.

"Old Woodward never got the credit for it, but here's what he did. He called Ford Frick, the president of the National League, and told him, 'Listen, I know what's happening. And I know you're sitting there figuring how you can pass the buck, as usual. Well, I think I am going to write a magazine piece for, say, Look or maybe the Saturday Evening Post, about how a cowardly league president will let this happen. That's what I'll do, Ford—unless, of course, you get off your ass and stop it. In which case I will throw that magazine piece into the garbage can and never mention it again.'

"So that's why Frick immediately issued a statement warning the Cardinals that every one of them would be suspended if they walked out. The world said what a wonderful man Frick was, and I guess Frick blushed with pride and took a bow.

"So Jackie was allowed to keep on keepin' on. And in October, he was voted the major-league Rookie of the Year.

"The Phillies had a manager named Ben Chapman who used to stand on the dugout steps and yell 'Nigger, nigger' at Jackie every time they played. And when they played down in Philly at Connie Mack Stadium, some of the crowd shouted right along with him. I guess when they awarded Jackie that hunk of major-league hardware, that shut old Ben Chapman's foul mouth with a crash."

"There's something else you should know about Jackie," the old ballplayer told his grandson. "In 1951, after Bobby Thomson hit the home run in the Polo Grounds that beat the Dodgers for the pennant, the stunned Dodgers turned and walked away—all but one. Off at the edge of the infield, Jackie stood all alone with his arms folded across his chest as his eyes followed Thomson's feet on their path around the bases. First . . . second . . . third . . . home.

"Only when he was satisfied that Thomson had touched each base, leaving no possible appeal to the umpires, did Robinson turn and walk away. He competed right down to the last second."

"Tell the boy this," Josh said. "I admit that sometimes we feel like he should have expressed a debt to the Negro Leagues and our managements, but that's because we feel so intensely, and he didn't go through that part with us. Hell, he only played half a season for the Monarchs. But nobody ever wanted to win a baseball game, any baseball game, more.

"Agreed," the old ballplayer said. "It's only right to say that the same fire for the game we had burned just as brightly in his belly."

"Yeah," Josh said, "but some folks never learned. I'm telling this to you because the boy is too young now, but someday when he's grown, I want you to repeat this to him.

"You remember Joe Cronin, and the way he treated Jackie and the others at that fake tryout when he managed the Red

Sox? Well, at the 1972 World Series, between the Reds and the A's, they planned to honor Jackie on the 25th anniversary of letting us play what they called the American game.

"He was losing his eyesight to diabetes. And he didn't live much longer. The plan was for the commissioner and the presidents of the two leagues to stand with Jackie at the pitcher's mound just before the game.

"Bowie Kuhn, the commissioner, sent Monte Irvin to get Cronin, who was the president of the American League. When Irvin found him, he was eating peanuts under the grandstand. 'Tell them I won't be there,' Cronin told him. 'Tell them I'm too busy.'

"Right," the ghost said to his old comrade, and seemingly to anyone who would listen. "Too busy to join the 20th century."

Chapter 12
The King of Mogmog

They were looking at a huge body of water. As it rolled toward them and then undulated its way back out, the boy bent over and clutched his stomach.

"I don't feel good, Pop Pop," he said. "I think I might upchuck."

"Take a deep breath, boy," the old ballplayer said. He rubbed Jeffy's back. "Where does it hurt you?"

Josh unleashed a burst of booming laughter. "He'll be fine in a couple of minutes, Jet. It's to be expected. Doesn't this scene feel a little different from all the others? Look closer and you'll see why." He pointed a gnarled finger. "That's the Pacific Ocean out there. The boy thinks he's seasick."

The old ballplayer stared out the window at the thunderous waves. "Damn you, can't you tell a simple story without all these theatrics?"

"This story ain't a bit simple, and you damn well know it," the ghost retorted. "But since you asked, the answer is no. These ain't sound effects, Jet. We in Ulithi, in the Caroline Islands, 900 miles from Iwo Jima. We headed for the dock at Mogmog, one of forty-nine islets in Ulithi. Long after we both dead and gone, this is gonna be part of the Federated States of Micronesia."

"We don't need no geography lesson," the old ballplayer said angrily. "You made my grandson sick, so this ain't a bit funny. Unless one day this collection of coral and Lord knows what else is gonna join the National League, what the hell we doin' here?"

"We come to see an old friend," Josh said. "At least, he will be after he leaves here. And don't you worry about the boy—right now he's fascinated by that school of yellowfin tuna swimming by. He won't upchuck. Did you know that yellowfin tuna's bodies are warmer than the water they swim in?"

"Damn it, Josh, get to the point, and the dock, before we fall out the window and drown."

"Well, let me explain one thing," the ghost said coolly. "No, the white leagues ain't comin' here. But pretty soon a little piece of Mogmog is going to improve the complexion of the American League. And after he shows them a thing or two, that group of elitists ain't never gonna be the same.

"This is 1945, Jet, the last year of World War II. Uncle Sam turned all of Ulithi into a Navy staging place for the invasion of Japan that was never necessary. They put more ships here for repairs and refitting and refueling than Pearl Harbor could berth, and it's way closer to Japan.

"They brought about 8,000 Marines and sailors and Seabees in, built everything they wanted, and evacuated the natives to other parts of the islands. Now tell the boy to look to the southeast over there at the two baseball fields. See the one closest? Now look at the batter."

"I know him. I mean, I really know him," the old ballplayer told the boy. "See the way he holds the bat ear-high before he drops it down? And the straight-up power of his body all melts into the short stride that was his signature. When that bat hits the ball, it isn't a question of 'if' but rather of 'how far.' Wait—see that?" He pointed toward the pitcher, who slumped, hands to hips, on the mound. "He knows that ball is outta here and off into the ocean behind center field.

"There . . . now he's rounding third for home. Musta been a walk-off home run to end the game. His name is Larry Doby, and he doesn't know it yet, but one day he will rewrite the history of the American League as the first black man to play in it. The man waiting at home plate to shake his hand is a major-league player who got himself drafted in the Navy. His name is Mickey Vernon, and he was and will again be the best hitter on the Washington Senators.

"Doby once told me that when he was only eleven he was playing with a semipro team of mill workers and former minor-leaguers in Camden, South Carolina," Jet said. "When he was 15, he was a starter on the most prestigious all-black team in Paterson, New Jersey—the Smart Set. He even played for my Eagles at 17 under the name of Larry Walker to stay eligible for a basketball scholarship from LIU.

"But when he was growing up, like you and me he never even dreamed of major-league baseball, never gave it a thought —it was out of the question for a black man," the ghost interjected. "But now, on the day you're seeing, everything is different. I want the boy to hear his conversation with Vernon."

Vernon: "You hear Armed Forces Radio last night? The Dodgers signed Jackie Robinson."

Doby: "Hell, yeah. And it got me to thinking that just maybe—well, are you gonna write that letter?"

Vernon: "Not gonna—I already did."

Josh let the picture fade out. "You remember I told you," he asked, "how Vernon wrote to Clark Griffith, the owner of the Senators?"

"Yeah," the old ballplayer said after repeating the story to the boy —and Jeffy reminded him that Griffith said he had no interest in hiring a black player.

Josh interrupted again. "Well, somebody else did. So we headin' back to Chicago now. The boy is gonna learn that Jackie's spectacular debut didn't exactly make everything right."

The old ballplayer told the boy, "Now you're going to learn all about my old teammate Larry Doby. When he came back from the Navy, he rejoined the Eagles under his own name. He hit .360, convinced he just might move on to organized baseball, what with Jackie already playing in Montreal. That year, we beat the Monarchs in the World Series and Jackie led Montreal to a pennant.

"Doby didn't know it, but that same year he was being scouted in almost every game on the orders of Bill Veeck, the man who owned the Cleveland Indians. I remember on July 4th we played a doubleheader in Washington against the Homestead Grays, and before the game we found out that Larry's contract had been sold to the Indians.

"He played the first game and hit his 15th home run of the year. That afternoon, his final Negro League batting average was .414. I recall we all chipped in and bought him a toilet kit! Abe Manley, the co-owner, said, 'Good luck, see you around,' and Larry headed for a world where he would be alone and lonely for longer than most people think.

"As the train rattled through the night," Jet went on, "he thought of what he had left behind . . . teammates like Leon Day and Len Pearson, and a remarkable 51-year-old catcher-manager named Biz Mackey . . . a social haven called the Grand Hotel on West Market Street where Negro League players were kings and the good times rolled each night.

"I don't think anyone could have been prepared for what happened to him the next day."

The scene outside the old bus windows shifted to Comiskey Park, where they had seen the East-West Negro League All-Star game earlier in the trip. The Indians were there to play the White Sox. Veeck was waiting for Doby outside the park.

Josh funneled the audio into the bus. Bill Veeck spoke to Larry Doby in much the same way that Branch Rickey had tutored Jackie Robinson.

"You know what we are getting into," Veeck was telling Doby. "Different hotels than the rest of the team, and most times even different restaurants. As bad as things will be in the National League for Robinson, they will be worse for you. I can't say that enough—we are talking two different leagues here. From a social standpoint, this league thinks it's better than anyone else." His look sharpened. "You and I are in this together. I will try as hard as I can to help you, but the negatives have to be dealt with. You can't get into a fight. You have to take whatever they give you and turn the other cheek."

While he was speaking, Lou Boudreau, the Indians' manager, who didn't want Doby in the first place, joined them.

"Introduce him to everyone," Veeck told Boudreau.

Josh broke in on the unfolding tale. "Boudreau could have done what Leo Durocher later did when Monte Irvin and Hank Thompson joined the Giants as their first African-Americans," the ghost said. "They walked in, and Leo shouted, 'Listen up, fellows! We have two new guys joining this team. I want to make it clear that I don't give a damn whether they are black, white, or Chinese. If they can help us win the pennant, I want them.' Then he walked away and everyone went about their business. There was no fuss.

"But I want to show you how Boudreau handled this same

thing," Josh added. "And then you tell me if he really wanted Larry."

The scene shifted again. They were looking into the Indians' locker room. Boudreau lined up the players in front of their lockers and introduced Doby one by one. At the very first locker, Doby held out his hand for the guy to shake. The guy said nothing, just turned his back, leaving Doby standing there with his hand extended in midair. It was that way all down the line. Only three guys—Bill McKechnie, a coach, Joe Gordon, the second baseman, and Jim Hegan, the catcher—offered genuine handshakes.

The old ballplayer and the boy watched as Doby changed into his new uniform. He walked slowly down the tunnel leading to the dugout. They could hear the familiar sounds of small groups playing pepper and baseballs tossed back and forth into gloves.

Doby stood on the top step, the loneliest man in all of Cleveland. Here he was on the brink of the biggest single moment of his life, and he might as well have been in Murmansk.

Nobody would throw him a ball.

"Look at those bastards," Josh muttered. But the old ballplayer wasn't listening—he was looking at Doby and feeling his pain.

Suddenly a guy was pulling Doby's elbow.

"Hey, rookie," Joe Gordon said with a big smile. "You gonna stand there and profile in your new uniform, or do you want to warm up?"

Jeffy was absorbed. "Mr. Gordon is a really nice guy," he murmured to his grandfather.

"Don't ever forget him and what he did—and most of the others and what they didn't do," the old ballplayer replied.

Josh picked up the story. "Doby was used as a pinch hitter," he said. "He struck out and returned to his seat in the dugout, far away from his manager. The next day, Boudreau told him he wanted him to start at first base. He had never played the position in his life. The first baseman refused to loan him his glove. The Indians' traveling secretary walked across the field and borrowed one for him from the White Sox.

"The circumstances grew beyond humiliation," the ghost went on. "In one game, Boudreau sent him up to pinch-hit for Dale Mitchell, who was already at bat. The count on Mitchell was 0-2. What does that say? That they all wore the same uniforms, but not all of them behaved like teammates. Before the isolation portion of his major-league career ended, he slid into second base at Philadelphia and the shortstop spit tobacco juice in his face. The knockdown pitches were thrown not high and tight to move him off the plate, but behind him—to where a batter normally ducks away."

With real anger, Josh added, "It wasn't the five or six inches closest to the plate that a lot of throwers were after. It was his head."

"We had an Eagles reunion years later," the old ballplayer said, "and he told me that in Washington he had to walk to the park in uniform with his spikes in his hand. And in St. Louis, well, he said that was the absolute worst."

The scene morphed again. They were in Sportsman's Park in St. Louis. Doby was kneeling in the batter's circle when a fan in the second row stood up. Doby knew the voice—he'd hit two home runs that day, and after each the man was on his feet screaming, "Nigger! Nigger!"

Doby went to bat. He popped up. As he headed back to the dugout, the fan started to yell vile obscenities about Doby's wife. Doby, furious, sprinted straight for the railing. He got one leg over it, and suddenly Indians coach Bill McKechnie, moving so quickly he was a blur in visitors' gray, hurled himself at Doby. He grabbed him around the waist and threw him to the ground.

The boy and the old ballplayer heard the coach scream, "You can't do that! Calm down—this league hates your guts! If you go up there, you are gone, and we won't get another black player for ten years."

The old ballplayer draped an arm over the boy's shoulder. "He just saved Larry's career," Jet said matter-of-factly. "He just saved it for all of us. Hell, when you think about it, he saved it for America. That same year, Larry became the first black ballplayer to hit a home run in a World Series."

"It took thirty-nine years before they put Larry Doby in the Hall of Fame," the ghost said. "But he never lost faith in himself or in the game he loved. He could have been bitter. He could have said so many negative things about what he went through. Now I want you to hear what he believed with the passing of time.

"The night before his Hall of Fame induction, he was walking with a reporter through the empty museum. Their wives were sitting in the lobby. The dimmed lights cast an eerie shadow over the exhibits. They were virtually alone in the building. The silence was broken only by the echo of their footprints down empty halls. They came to an exhibit featuring the Indians' 1948 World Series triumph. Doby stared silently at the team photo, and then he turned his attention to the one next to it: a black-and-white Associated Press photo of Doby and a pitcher named Steve Gromek embracing.

Then Doby spoke.

'That picture ran in every paper in the country—a guy who happened to be white and a guy who happened to be black embracing in victory. I don't think there was ever a picture like that on the front page of a newspaper anywhere in the South. America needed a picture like that. I'll always be proud I could be part of giving this country that moment."

In a tone tinged with both reverence and bitterness, Josh said, "A great player, black, white, or Chinese."

Chapter 13
The Battle of Pittsburgh

The ghost was silent, which in itself was among the strangest things that had happened since the journey began. Twice the old ballplayer had spoken to him and twice the ghost, deep in thought for a while, had waved him off.

"I've had about enough of your hoodoo-superiority nonsense," the old ballplayer said. "I already admitted that you were the best hitter I ever saw . . . . But it's about time you remembered that I played against you—you was great, but you wasn't no Superman. I appreciate the time you takin' with my grandson, but, damn, I seen you on days when you wasn't exactly Babe Ruth. So get past that down mood and tell me what's next."

"That's not right, Pop Pop," Jeffy interrupted. "Mr. Gibson has taught me a lot, and I think—"

"—listen, boy," Jet cut in. "Think about what you just said. You sticking up for a piece of floating jelly you can't even see or hear!"

"Hold it right there, old fool!" Josh stepped up. "I may be dead, but at least the boy knows I ain't insensitive. He's got more sense than you. I been quiet because we're heading back to a place that's the closest thing I ever had to home, seein' how much time I spent on the road.

"We going to Pittsburgh, to the Land of Cumberland Posey and Gus Greenlee. It's a place where they never disrespected me, a place where us colored folk had not one but two Negro major-league teams. Think about that. Cincinnati didn't have two big-league white teams. Neither did Washington. Back when we played, white folks in Baltimore didn't have no major-league team at all."

He drew a ghostly breath. "But Pittsburgh was the soul of black baseball. Don't talk to me about Kansas City and the Monarchs. No wonder they won nine straight Negro American League pennants. The Homesteads and the Crawfords and the Elite Giants and the Cubans and the New York Black Yankees and the Newark Eagles didn't play in the Monarchs' league."

"Well, you could be right about that," the old ballplayer said. "But I still can't quite see what makes Pittsburgh so big a deal. What about Chicago?"

"Look out that window, Jet," the ghost replied. "That's Homestead, Pennsylvania, in 1930. And that's the Monongahela River. Those smokestacks right at its edge are the U.S. Steel Homestead Works. Now cross the city limits to Pittsburgh"—his finger traced the journey—"and that section over there we called the Hill. That's just 4.7 miles from Homestead.

"The Hill was the heartbeat of black Pittsburgh. Homestead was what drove a lot of our people's economy, and on that line between Homestead and the Hill, Cumberland Posey and Gus Greenlee fought the greatest rivalry in all of black baseball. Tell the boy that."

"I never heard of those men," the boy said after the old ballplayer relayed the ghost's story. "Did you know them?"

"Oh, yes, I knew them. Cum Posey was the son of a black

riverboat pilot. He took the Grays, a mill-town semipro team, to the threshold of greatness. Gus Greenlee over in Pittsburgh did the same for the Pittsburgh Crawfords. Those two teams were the Dodgers and Giants of black baseball. Each had the team the other loved to beat."

"I played for both of them," Josh added. "I lived on the Hill. I'm here to tell you that there never was a rivalry like that one. But first I got to show you the power of the man who was and still is a legend on the Hill and over in Homestead . . . A man who lived among the people and starred for both of their teams." He pointed to the east. "Look over there. That's Ammon Field."

Ammon Field was where the twin legends of the Crawfords and the Grays put down shared roots. When the Crawfords started there, it was a city-owned, poorly maintained field. The Grays, in the meantime, were paying outrageous rent at Forbes Field but were not allowed to dress in the Pirates' locker room.

The old ballplayer, his grandson, and the ghost found themselves standing next to one of the crude dugouts looking out toward second base, where a man in a Crawford uniform was crawling around on his hands and knees.

"Why is that man doing that?" the boy asked.

"I'll answer that," the old ballplayer told the ghost. "I played enough games on this field as an Eagle to know exactly what he's doing. His name is Charlie Hughes. There's a drain-pipe that runs under this field. Apart from the hard-packed earth that could alter the course of a grounder, the pipe was barely beneath the surface. Occasionally if the ball bounced off its outline, it would carom sideways. Charlie Hughes would play that carom like Minnesota Fats lining up an 8-ball shot to a corner pocket. Robbed me more than once."

At that point, the ghost waved his hands twice. The view

faded out and then morphed into a June afternoon in 1930. The Keystones, a local black team that would soon disappear, were hosting the Crawfords at Ammon. The batter stepping in to hit was a young catcher playing his first game for the Crawfords.

The catcher had roots on both sides of the great Posey-Greenlee divide. The kid worked at the Westinghouse Air Brakes Factory in Pittsburgh while his father worked across the divide at the Homestead Mill. The Crawfords were beginning to challenge the Grays for local popularity, and on this day five thousand fans packed every seat and standing-room spot at Ammon.

"Watch this young man hit," the ghost said. "This is his first at-bat for the Crawfords. See how he swings, how the ball explodes off his bat. It's why infields always played deep on him. His line drives could take your head off.

"Now follow that ball—if you can. Look how it soars over Ammon Field Hill, climbs past the tennis courts behind and into a group of houses beyond.

"Got four hits that day, and we just about chased the Keystones out of town. That was the start that changed the Crawfords from a little local team to the monsters that challenged Cum Posey's Homestead Grays."

His grin broadened. "Now watch the young catcher's victory trot around the bases."

"Pop Pop," the boy said, jumping up and down in excitement. "I think that's Mr. Gibson."

Josh boomed his explosive laugh. "Yes, it is! It's me. And don't I look just fine?"

Then the old school bus seemed to rock back and forth. Somehow, to Jet, it signaled that an important moment was coming.

"I think," he said, "we're about to see Cum Posey and Gus Greenlee in action. Boy, this is serious stuff. These guys were to our community what Stoneham and Mack and Wrigley and Comiskey were to all-white baseball. Hell, they were even more. A year later, after working a few menial jobs, Gus started a bootlegging business and ran it from out of a taxi. That gave him more money to invest in his ball club. Then, along came a local barber named Weegie Harrris. His barbershop was a thriving front for his real occupation, as one of the town's numbers kings. He became a silent partner with Gus—and money ceased to be a problem. The silence was necessary: Greenlee did not want the cops to poke into his ball club's revenue.

This was the capital of Gus Greenlee's fiefdom. There was the Savoy ballroom, upstairs above the Royal Theater, and, finally, there was the Crawford Grill at Wylie and Townsend. This was the classiest place in the neighborhood, and the neighborhood was home to the classiest action on the Hill.

The old ballplayer broke the reverie. "Visiting ballplayers stayed around the corner at the Ellis Hotel. The town, and the Crawford, were both noted for the jazz musicians they attracted. You could see them all: Ahmad Jamal, Earl "Fatha" Hines, Roy Eldridge, Art Blakey . . . boy, I could go on forever."

"You usually do," Josh interjected. "Right now, look through that window there in the Crawford Grill. Tell the boy that the big fella over there by the bar with the cigar is Gus Greenlee. He is about to challenge the Homestead Grays to see who owns Pittsburgh.

"Listen to him."

"Everybody wants to know why the Crawfords ain't played the Grays yet. Well, hell, it's because that little ol' semipro team I bought sure wasn't ready. But it is now.

"By next year I'm gonna sign Cool Papa Bell, Jimmy Crutchfield, Boojun Wilson, John Henry Russell, Leroy Matlock, Judy Johnson, Rap Dixon. And it may take a year or two to find that rascal who keeps moving around, but I'm also gonna sign Satchel Paige. I am talking about what will become the greatest damn black team of the 1930s and maybe beyond.

"You think I'm too quick to put down the Grays because they been top dog around here for a long time? Well, I got two more hole cards here. I'm gonna build me my own stadium: Greenlee Field, first Negro-owned ballpark in the U S of A. Gonna build it over near Ammon . . . grandstand, lights and all . . . and before I'm done, the Grays will be renting playing time from me."

"Well," a member of his entourage at the bar put in, "that's mighty impressive, but if you ain't got a local star . . ."

"Oh, I got a local star," Greenlee cut in. "Gonna be the most local and the most star on the Hill. I got the black Babe Ruth, a catcher named Josh Gibson, who gonna be playin' for me on the Hill for a long, long time. Because when the Grays steal him—and they will—I'm gonna steal him right back."

"Huh," the ghost snorted as the images dissolved. "Black Babe Ruth? He always did have a little bullshit in his line. He needs to be saying that the Babe was the white Josh Gibson."

"How many times you gonna say that, Josh? Why don't you show the boy Cum Posey—because in the end he won the battle and the city. And like you said, you played for both of them."

"You right for once. For this, the scene shifts over to Homestead."

The old ballplayer had made that trip many times during his career, but he had forgotten how much Homestead was like the Hill. Like the Lower and Upper Hill, it was divided by class and race. Sixth was a chain of saloons, houses, pawn shops, and pool halls. Most of the neighborhood's black citizens lived in the ward and worked as domestics or laborers. Those better off lived higher on the hillside.

Posey was a trailblazer. As a young man he played basketball for Penn State, rare for a black man, and he was one of America's best college players. He thought big and sometimes acted bigger.

At the time, he had already signed an aging but famous pitcher named Smokey Joe Williams. Posey was shaping the nucleus that Greenlee planned to steal. That year, the Grays won more than one hundred games. That spurred Posey to add a group of Negro League All-Star players. He signed future Hall of Famers Cool Papa Bell, Judy Johnson, Willie Foster, and Martín Dihigo. He also stole Greenlee's catcher, Josh Gibson.

When the Grays signed Oscar Charleston, they became one of the best teams of the era, black or white. Like the Crawfords, they were still a semipro team. Ironically, the man who would make them full professionals happened to be Gus Greenlee, who re-formed the defunct Negro National League and invited Posey in as a charter member.

But to get his stars, Posey needed a bankroll, the ghost told them as they walked down Sixth Street. "There he is, on the corner," Josh said. "He's talking to his new 'banker.' The guy's name is Rufus Sonny Man Johnson.

"You won't regret it," Posey was saying. "Homestead is gonna have the classiest team in all of colored baseball. I can sign those guys and when I do I'm gonna get us brand-new Buicks. We gonna travel to the games with the same class that we going to play them with.

"And I'll tell you this," he added to Sonny Man. "You may own the best nightclub in town, the Sky Rocket. You may be the king of the numbers this side of Pittsburgh. But I promise you that one day you will be known as the man who made the Homestead Grays America's finest black baseball team."

"I wouldn't tell that to too many folks if I was you," Sonny Man replied. "I mean about me needing to remain a silent partner and all. You best think that part a little bit more."

"Got that," Posey said. "Square business."

But in 1932, Greenlee retaliated in a way that immediately made his Crawfords number one in Pittsburgh, and he kept his promise to their fans.

He did sign Oscar Charleston, and Judy Johnson, and Cool Papa Bell, Jimmy Crutchfield, Ted "Double Duty" Radcliffe, and Josh Gibson. Most of them were lured and signed from Posey's "finest colored team in America."

And then he got Satchel.

Old-timers on the Hill said the party that night at the Crawford, which may have lasted several nights, was one for the ages.

Suddenly, Pittsburgh became a verbal battlefield much like the New York megalopolis when sidewalk debates on soft summer nights centered around who was best, Mickey, Willie, or the Duke. On the Hill, it was "you think Posey can beat that team of Greenlee's? No way." The statement never went unchallenged.

Ammon Field had become too small. Forbes Field was too costly for Posey. So Greenlee stepped in and opened Greenlee Field.

"I could see the difference, and so could Pittsburgh's black folks," Josh told his travelers. "I mean, when black families went to see the Grays at Forbes Field, they dressed for it, just like the whites who went there. Women looked fine, men with white shirts and ties."

"That's right," the old ballplayer said. "But at Greenlee, it was more like a Southern barbecue. Those fans raised hell, and they bet—Lord, did they bet. They bet a quarter on what pitch, or what field it would be hit to, or third strikes. Eventually the Grays played a lot of games there, too, before they moved half your home games to Washington."

As the fog rolled in again, the ghost looked back at the Hill. "Lord, " he said, "I miss this place. I played here. I lived not far from the ballpark. I spent long nights at the Crawford Bar and Grill. I danced a time or two at Savoy.

"And for a glorious time, I caught Satch—right here at Ammons and right there at Greenlee, and even at Forbes. He had a great variety of pitches and he had names for each one. The one I liked best was the Hesitation Pitch, where he would go into a windmill and pause a split second at the very top, and when he did that and held the ball up there, every unmarried lady in the place shouted the kind of oohs and ahhs they generally reserved for the bedroom."

"Why did you say that Mr. Greenlee lost the battle with Mr. Posey?" the boy asked.

"You best not tell your mother we talked about gambling," Jet said with a smile. "But what happened was that the police chief, Gus' good friend, got removed from office, and the next one was not a Greenlee fan. They shut him down and he went broke. That put him out of baseball, and it put Greenlee Field out, period. They tore it down."

"Maybe he shouldn't have been in the numbers racket," the boy said.

Jet and Josh both laughed.

"Well, things were different back then," Jet told the boy. "Booking numbers was a gambling operation, but the black community looked at it a little differently. To begin with, the neighborhoods played the numbers looking for a windfall that their jobs couldn't give them. Second, the guys who ran the numbers banks in the big cities were kind of heroic in their neighborhood—I can't begin to tell you how much they did for families whose kids needed college money, or maybe food. But you had to be there in those days to understand that."

He nodded toward Josh. "It would be hard," the old ballplayer said, "to find a Negro League team owner who wasn't doing the numbers."

Chapter 14
The One, the Only Satchel

The old ballplayer was lost in thought. His eyes were closed as the boy beside him slept with his head in his grandfather's lap. Jet was thinking about his daughter, the boy's mom, and what he would have to explain to her eventually. The boy had never spent a night anywhere but in their own home. He had never been separated from her for even a full day. But now, without her permission, and without her knowledge, the grandfather had taken her son on a journey that was either a dream or an adventure (which one, he did not know) and let it override the obvious truth that he would have some tough explaining to do.

He knew she was her mother's daughter in every way. He also knew their unexplained absence would cause the girl fierce pain, so there would come an inevitable confrontation.

He dreaded the thought of it. He dreaded the certainty that the look of betrayal in her eyes would reflect those of her late mother, on the few occasions he had hurt her. How in the world could he tell her something inane like "the ghosts made me do it"?

He reached out to caress the boy's cheek when suddenly he was jolted from his reverie by the sound of a nasty argument.

"Damn it, get the hell off this bus! This is my shift and my story, so you get out right now!"

Jet knew it in his heart—there was no mistaking that voice: Satchel Paige had arrived on the scene.

"Oh, really? So why didn't they send you down here right at the start? I'll tell you why. It's because you can't be trusted. You walked out on the Monarchs for a few dollars before the seventh game of the World Series, and they lost . . . You walked out on the Crawfords years before that for a week to play with white boys for a white boy's paycheck in North Dakota . . . You—"

"—just hold on there, boy, because you damn well know the truth," the old ballplayer heard Josh retort. "You and I were heroes to our people. They knew there weren't no white boys anywhere who could play this game better than us. But we weren't heroes to the people who owned our teams. They nickel-and-dimed us to death. If you got the same offers I did, you woulda done the same damn thing."

"And I got them because I was the king who put the people in the ballpark. You was a great hitter, Josh, probably the best who ever lived. But you wasn't no pitcher, and a pitcher of my caliber—of which I think there were no others—could carry a team and draw a crowd all by himself.

"I will admit," Paige's voice added, "that nobody ever hit home runs that went as far as yours. I know that. I know about the 500-footer in Cuba and the one even longer in Pennsylvania. I know those smart baseball historians still argue about whether you was the first and onliest one to actually hit the ball out of the old Yankee Stadium or whether it landed in the bullpen.

"Nobody could hit a baseball as far as you—that includes those cheatin' steroid guys who will come along in the future.

"Don't mess with me, Josh! You know the boys sent me

down to tell my story to this little boy. And they didn't put no restrictions on me. No mumbo-jumbo ghost jive where he can't see or hear me for my part in this trip. No more of this feeling sorry for the great colored hitter the white world didn't appreciate.

"And no hiding things from the boy we all chose to be our messenger! He'll be able to ask me straight up without having to throw Jet here any damn thing he wants.

"After the Negro Leagues, I won in their major leagues. I pitched in their World Series. I was the first black man to get into their Hall of Fame. So you best go on home now for a while. You was a great player, but the boys have decided that it's my turn to be this young man's tour guide. My turn now. And his granddaddy played against me, just as you did.

"So, get off the bus. For a little while anyway, it's gonna be my show completely."

After silence took over, the old ballplayer gently shook the boy awake.

Josh was gone. In his place sat Satchel Paige. The fog outside the window revealed the rural hills of Alabama.

"Don't get nervous, son," Satchel told the boy. "It's really me. And you need to hear my story from me. Tell him, Jet. I'll even give you an autograph later. But right now I want you to look out there and read that sign for me."

Jeffy's face reflected surprised happiness at this latest visit. He nodded to the new ghost. "I can do that, Mr. Paige," he said with some excitement. "The sign says 'Mount Meigs Campus of the Industrial School for Negro Children.'"

"Smart boy," Satchel said with a grin. "But that sign lies. That sign is Jim Crow shorthand for saying 'where we put uppity colored kids.' You might call it a colored reform school. Now look yonder. That's the baseball field. That fellow in the sweatshirt is named Edward Byrd. See that tall all-arms-and-legs colored boy? That's me—the great Leroy Robert 'Satchel' Paige.

"Now look at Byrd—and listen to him."

"Try again, Leroy," Coach Byrd said. "Kick that front foot higher . . . higher . . . higher than that. Swing your arm around at an angle so that it looks to the batter like that big hand of yours is gonna hit him right smack in his face. Now do it again . . . and again . . . again. You do that every afternoon you come out to this ball field and I promise you, with what I have seen, you are going to be the Man every time you step on that mound—no matter where it is, no matter how old you are, no matter who you pitchin' against and what uniform you're wearing.

"Mr. Byrd," the gangly boy said, "I have always been a first baseman, and . . ."

"Get that out your head, Leroy. You a pitcher, startin' now and forever."

Satch laughed. So did the boy and the old ballplayer. "Well," Satch spoke up. "They turned me loose from that institution, as I recollect, long 'bout 1923, and a fellow name of R.T. Jackson signed me for the Birmingham Black Barons. I struck out 18 against the colored Nashville Giants—no white pitcher could equal that record in either of 'their' leagues until 1938, when Bob Feller did it for the Cleveland Indians.

"But the big thing, what I think pissed Josh off the most, if you heard our little argument, was that Mr. Jackson came up with this idea to rent me out and give me a piece of the rent money. Josh never had that extra income. The fact that I finally pitched in the majors angered him—that and the fact he never got there.

"In 1930, R.T. leased me to the Baltimore Black Sox. So I was learning how to make a little more money than the other guys, because the owners understood I was the reason more people came to the games. I was from the South, and guys on the team were, you might say, city slickers. They didn't care much for my accent and style of conversatin'. But I took the money. After that season, I was gone.

"A year later, I pitched in a city that also had a white major-league team," Satch went on. "I pitched for the colored Cleveland Buckeyes, in the shadow of the Cleveland Indians' ballpark. It pissed me off all year. They Jim Crowed me out of any chance to pitch in that other park, but I knew I was better than anything they had.

"Now, this may sound like a monologue," he added with a very Satchel smile. "But I'm not Josh, and there's things you got to know, and I am the onliest one who can tell you. I understand Josh carried you all over to Pittsburgh. Well, I played for both of those teams. Played against Josh and with Josh.

"I pitched just about everywhere. People up at Cooperstown say I pitched in more than 2,500 games. Nearest they can tell, I won about 2,000 of them. With three hundred shutouts, fifty-five no-hitters. One stretch, I pitched twenty-nine games in a single month. Don't recall what I did on the two days I took off.

"So, yeah, I learned early to go where the money was. I jumped the Crawfords and went to Bismarck for a short time to play with a white-boys amateur team and made good money up there. Then back to the Crawfords . . . played in Cuba and the Dominican Republic . . . in Mexico and Puerto Rico and Venezuela and Canada. Hell, to make the rent I woulda gone to Transylvania if they had a team there.

"One time there was this black teams' charity doubleheader at Yankee Stadium. I drove all night from Pittsburgh, parked near the stadium, and fell asleep. They sent a batboy out to look for me. He banged on the window to wake me up, scared the hell out of me. So we ran down to the stadium and I got dressed just in time to start the first game. I pitched all the way through extra innings until they called it for darkness, when we was tied 1-1.

"Boy, I beat DiMaggio and Dean and Feller in barnstorming games. DiMaggio called me the best pitcher he ever faced. I loved to hear the white boys say things like that. I even had me a DC-3—painted on the side was 'Satchel Paige All-Stars.'"

Satchel finally paused for a breath. Jet chimed in: "The fog outside the window is still there. Are you sure you know what you're doing?"

"Relax, Jet," Satch answered with a grin. "It's time to have a little fun. Look out there. What you see now is called Dexter Park, home of one of the greatest semipro teams in the country: the Bushwicks. Lot of those fellas played in the majors once upon a time, and a lot of others were headed there in the future.

"Just look at that crowd for a semipro game. Damn, this place is packed. You wanna know why? They knew I was pitchin' so they turned out—couldn't get another skinny ass into the joint. That happened wherever I pitched.

"Lemme show you. Look over there, that tall young guy warming up. Look at his form. Look at his style, at that leg kick. You know who that is, boy?"

"Well, I'm not sure," the boy said, "but it looks a lot like you."

"Hey, Jet!" Satch said to the old ballplayer after a big laugh. "You got one smart grandson here. Yeah, boy, that's the great Satchel Paige himself—or I should say myself."

He paused, clearly relishing the setup he was about to present. "Now, that young boy coming up to hit—yeah, he's green now and he's got a lot to learn, but one day he's going to be the starting shortstop for the New York Yankees and eventually a Hall of Famer. Fans all over America will know him as the Scooter. His real name is Phil Rizzuto."

The tableau that Satch unveiled for the boy looked like this:

Rizzuto dug in. He saw the leg kick and the hand coming at him from an angle, and he let the pitch go by.

Strike one.

The next one was the crowd-pleaser he invented: the hesitation pitch. There is a furious windmill windup and then the pause at the top of the arc, followed by a myriad of what seems like flailing arms and legs jumping out at the batter, and then a split-second pause at the top of the arc. Followed by a flaming darter.

Strike two.

And now Satch's clone grinned down from the mound at the future Yankee as if to say, "Watch this one, kid. Nothing complicated. Just pure speed."

A sound made the boy turn toward the ghost. "Why are you laughing, Mr. Paige?" the boy asked, starting to laugh himself.

"Because I know I got him," Satch said. "Great pitchers always know. Now watch."

This time Rizzuto managed to swing. He missed by a foot.

Years later, a sportswriter asked Rizzuto, "Is it true you batted as a kid against Satch?"

"Sure did," Scooter answered, "but don't even ask me what he threw."

"Why not?"

"I couldn't tell you, because I didn't see one damn pitch."

"He was right about that," Satch said. He folded his hands behind his head. "You know, I did pitch in the majors. Your grandfather can tell you all about that. Made the Hall of Fame. Made the highest salary in the history of the Negro Leagues: $650 a month from the Crawfords. Made more money in winter ball in Latin America and barnstorming from Florida to Alaska against major-leaguers. I could generally make $40,000 any year, maybe three, four times more than any Yankee except DiMaggio."

The old ballplayer explained to the boy who Joe DiMaggio was.

"Mr. Gibson never talked about him," the boy said.

Satch broke in. "Well, maybe that's because he would've had to tell you about the success I had against the man the white folks called the Yankee Clipper." He slapped the boy lightly on the back. "Truth be told, Josh doesn't want to give me much credit—he's still angry about what I did to him in the 1942 Negro Leagues World Series."

Satch drew their attention to the window again. "Look out there—that's Forbes Field in Pittsburgh. You can see what I mean. I'm pitchin' for the Kansas City Monarchs against the Crawfords. It's Game Two, and I'm protecting a lead. And I'm a little tired, as you can tell."

The boy and the old ball player watched intently as Paige gave up three straight singles. "The bases are loaded," Satch said, "and here comes Josh up to hit, looking at me like he's Jimmy Cagney and the bat is a tommygun."

Paige stepped off the mound and yelled something at Gibson.

"I just told him he was going down," Satch remembered with another laugh.

"That ain't the way I heard it," the old ballplayer responded. "I know you better than that, Satch. I heard you told him it was time for him to get ready to hear a little chin music and he better watch his ass."

"Shame on you, talkin' that way in front of this innocent boy here," Satch clowned in return. "Now butt out and let the boy watch!"

What unfolded was a duel between the best Negro League pitcher ever and the best Negro League hitter ever.

Twice Satch baited Josh low and away with curveballs, both almost unhittable. But Josh managed to make contact and foul them off. Now the same thought ran through both their minds: fastball.

Satch was ready to make it strength against strength. This was no World Series showdown. This was Satch against Josh for the championship of each other.

But this time, Satch was a little cuter. He came in on the inside corner and Josh had to protect the plate. The force of his missed swing sent him to his knees.

"See that, see that!" Satch said and laughed so hard the old bus seemed to tremble. "I never let him forget that."

"You know," the old ballplayer told the boy as the scene faded, "this is a remarkable man. He pitched in and won his first official American League game at age forty-two."

Satch grinned and nodded. "Stand up, boy," he said to Jeffy. "Turn around." Satch studied the youngster's physique. "Well, you sure ain't gonna be no pitcher. I'd say with those legs, when the time comes, you'll be an outfielder just like your grandfather and you will do some flyin' on those basepaths."

"How do you know I'll even play?" the boy asked.

"Oh, you'll play. I know, all right. Believe me on that."

Satch inclined his ghostly head as if listening. "Listen, boy, that old catcher is on his way back here right now. My time is just about up. Listen close. I want to explain something to you. The league—I mean the travel and the girls—can make a bum out of the best of us. One day when you're older you will have to deal with that. You will be a major-leaguer one day—so here's my advice for when you get there.

"Work like you don't need the money. Love like you've

never been hurt. Dance like nobody's watching. And don't look back, because somebody might be gaining on you.

"And right now, that somebody is Josh. Here he comes. So one last thing, boy. Ain't no man can avoid bein' born average. But there ain't no man got to be common. . . ."

Then Satchel Paige was gone. Josh Gibson had regained the bus.

Chapter 15
The Man on the Press Box Roof

"Where did Mr. Paige go?" the boy asked when he saw Josh had returned.

Josh Gibson looked at the ceiling with an expression that looked like he wanted to say, "Ask a stupid question, expect a stupid answer."

But then he saw the boy's trusting look. And he understood: Jeffy was seeing and hearing him, experiencing him, all for the first time. In their own very different ways, the old catcher and the young boy were realizing that their relationship and their mystic connection were evolving to a whole new place. The appearance of Satchel Paige, in the "onliest" way he knew how, had somehow made all that possible.

Josh felt in his heart that he had to answer the boy as though their "friendship" hadn't changed a bit. So he did.

"The way Satch moved around when he was playin'," he began, "he could be in Paris, France, for all I know—especially if there's a loose dollar a pitcher could scoop up over there.

"Well, that's not fair. It really was like he said. The owners we dealt with threw nickels around as though they were manhole covers. Satch was a far better businessman than the rest of us. Can't fault him about that. I just want to clear up one thing. I hit him as many times as he struck me out."

"Well, I like him," the boy said with some pride in his voice. He already seemed innocently comfortable with the fact that he was conversing with the ghost his grandfather had been "translating" up to then.

The grandfather laughed. "I see nothin' much has changed with Ol' Satch," he said. "Women and kids all loved him. So where are we headed now, Josh?"

"Well, if the boy's gonna be the chosen messenger for all of us, there's some folks he got to learn about who never played the game but still made it all happen."

"Will I see Mr. Paige again?" the boy asked.

"I 'spect so," the ghost replied. "That's not exactly the plan, but . . . trust him to turn up somewhere if he's determined to be there. I can't remember a time when he didn't do what the hell he wanted. He's a very strong-willed person and a strong-willed ghost. I guess that's what made him great. Now that he's gone, I will say that he was the greatest we ever had.

"But now, pay close attention to what happens next. Do you guys see that old man standing on the big wooden veranda porch of the Otesaga Hotel up there in Cooperstown? Recognize him, Jet?"

Once again, the fog had dissipated. The old man had no trouble discerning.

"Well, of course I do," he said with a wide smile. "That's Sam Lacy. There ain't a guy who played Negro League baseball who didn't read him at some time or other. He was fearless and fair."

He turned to the boy. "Do you remember when we watched the Washington Senators' Opening Day parade? When one of the players cursed at an old man and spit in his face? That old man never went to see another white man play ball. Well, Sam is his son, the young man we saw standing next to him.

"Sam was one of the most influential black men to write for any newspaper. He wrote for the Chicago Defender, the Pittsburgh Courier, the Baltimore Afro-American—those papers, all by themselves, spread the news about what black baseball was about. But what's he doing here in Cooperstown?"

"We're now well into the future, Jet," the ghost replied, "and the Baseball Writers' Association of America has voted to put him into the Hall of Fame's journalism wing at age 94. What does that have to say about how things are finally going to change?"

"About time!" the old ballplayer said. "I'll take it from here, Josh."

He launched a story for the boy. "Sam never did care much for the new computer technology. I guess by the time this happened to him in the future, arthritis came between him and his typewriter. For the last twenty years of his career, he wrote his columns longhand on a plain paper tablet. He drove the Beltway from Washington, where he lived, to Baltimore, where he worked for decades. When he got too old to drive, his son drove him. But Sam still went every day. He never retired.

"What Sam did was to tell his readers what otherwise might have remained a lot of silent truth. And he put it in perspective."

Josh waved a hand to silence him. "I'm gonna prove it in a way the boy will never forget. All right, close your eyes and count 1-2-3." A pause. "Now open them.

"We are in the room of a famous sportswriter, on the second floor of the Otesaga. He's sitting at the desk writing his column about Sam on a device of the future called a laptop computer. Look over his shoulder and read it out loud. Don't worry, he won't hear you."

The boy read:

"This is about Sam Lacy, an American sports columnist who happens to be an Afro-American. He has little tolerance for charades. Like it or not—and most of them do—he remains a mirror to the American reality, the journalistic eyes and ears of that community, providing a viewpoint it rarely gets anywhere else.

"For the white community—and, yes, at times, even the black—he has been the conscience they may not want to hear but are better off for having heard it. For more than six decades, he has been America's version of Diogenes with a deadline.

"He was there when Joe Louis and Jesse Owens rose above America's color prejudice inside the arena and was privy to the burdens American social mores laid on them when outside of it. He was there as a major force when Jackie Robinson and Larry Doby waged their lonely battles to shatter baseball's color line, only to discover he was just as isolated in his attempts to cover them from the press box.

"Long before it happened, he was the heavy artillery of this struggle."

"Don't forget that," the old ballplayer instructed the boy. Moments later, Gibson plucked them away and placed them back on the veranda, where five white sportswriters were interviewing Lacy.

"I thought the way to do it," Lacy was saying to the group, "was to embarrass them in the public print. I wrote to Kenesaw Mountain Landis, the commissioner of the lily-white baseball world, and asked for just ten minutes anywhere, anytime, any place, to prove baseball segregation was wrong. I never even got an answer.

"Later, I got appointed by baseball management to a new committee to study the possibility of integrating baseball. But the committee never met. Finally, a year after Jackie and Larry broke that line, I became the first black journalist to be accepted into the Baseball Writers' Association of America. They told me that the BBWAA card gets you into any press box in baseball."

The fog lifted, swirled. Then they were in a new venue.

"See that little ballpark down there?" Josh asked. "That's Pelican Stadium in New Orleans, and the Dodgers are about to play a preseason exhibition game. Sam has been covering them since Jackie Robinson joined the team the year before. So listen and watch."

The rooftop press box was surprisingly large. Even with the visiting press it will not be crowded. Like the other writers, mostly from New York and Cleveland, Sam Lacy had made the climb to it and was about to enter when the press-box custodian shoved the flat of his hand against Lacy's chest and said, "What the hell do you want, nigger?"

Sam Lacy never lost his cool. He reached into his back pocket, pulled out his wallet, and held out his Baseball Writers' Association of America press card.

The custodian kept his hand pressed against Lacy's chest. "Stick that card where the sun don't shine," he said.

"You don't understand. There are only two black players in all of major-league baseball, Jackie and Lary Doby, and they are both in this game," Lacy said in a controlled voice.

"I don't care if Marcus Garvey is playing shortstop," the man barked. "No nigger is coming into my press box."

He leaned back, his hand still planted on Sam's chest, and pulled a chair out of the first row. "Here's your damn seat. Now climb up to the roof of this press box and you can pretend you are a white sportswriter up there until football season, for all I care, and the wind blows you and your chair straight over the side."

Sam did what he was told—he wasn't going to let this redneck jerk keep him from doing his job.

The old ballplayer, the boy, and the ghost watched him make notes in his scorebook for three innings. Around the third inning, Lacy heard a commotion. He had visitors.

Three New York writers—Dick Young of the Daily News, Roscoe McGowan of the Times, and Bill Roeder of the World-Telegram and Sun—were schlepping across the roof, each dragging a chair behind him.

"What's going on?" Lacy asked.

"We need to get some sun," Young said.

"You fellows have been down at spring training for six weeks in Florida," Lacy said. "You don't need the sun. Dick, you look almost as dark as me."

The ghost chimed in. "They just stood up for Mr. Lacy and for a principle," the ghost said. "They were right. Sam was himself a man of principles, which is a good thing—without men of principles, nobody would ever know we played this game, much less let the whole game be integrated."

The old ballplayer nodded his agreement. "You know, Sam had principles whether the issue was black or white or yellow or brown. For him, right was right and wrong was wrong. Did you ever see his wife? You'd swear she was a white woman. I mean, she really was a colored lady, so I guess maybe another colored lady would know that from her hair, but she sure looked like Snow White to me."

"So Muhammad Ali one time came to Baltimore," the ghost continued. "Sam told the Nation of Islam brothers there that he would like to come to the mosque and present the champ with an award on behalf of the Afro-American newspaper. I know about this because all us boys who had passed on to heaven were looking down and we watched when he and his wife walked up the steps to the mosque, him with this big plaque from the Afro under his arm.

"They got to the door, and this guy in a Fruit of Islam uniform stopped them: "Mr. Lacy, you can come in, but that white lady can't."

The old ballplayer shook his head. "Didn't he explain that she really is a colored woman and she happened to be his wife?"

"Come on, think about that," the ghost said. "Think about what we know about Sam. He's thinkin', what if she really were white and his wife? He's thinkin' what an insult it was to do that to any woman under any circumstances."

"Did he argue and finally tell him who she was?" Jet asked.

"Come on, you know Sam. The way he dealt was to never lose his cool and, above all, be fair. So he said just one thing: 'Tell the champ I was here.'

"Then he took his wife's arm and they back down the steps about halfway. The guy was watching them. Sam waved, took the plaque, and left it right there on the steps. They kept walking and didn't look back. That's Sam."

To the old ballplayer's amazement, the change in the boy's relationship with the ghost—that they were now seeing and hearing each other—was clearly a source of enjoyment for both of them. Josh, defensive as he had been earlier, seemed almost exhilarated by the boy's company.

The ghost picked up his tale. "People," he said, "never understood how hard it was for the black writers to get respect from the people who ran the major leagues right down to the press-box attendants. They didn't understand that even the black men who covered our struggle had battles of their own once we began to cross over after Robinson and Doby. As part of their jobs as journalists, those writers had to follow us.

"You already saw Wendell Smith back in Boston when they

gave Jackie what turned out to be that fake tryout. Smith was the one who put the pressure on to make it happen. And when Jackie made the majors, Wendell was his ghost writer . . . Hey, 'ghost-wrote'—now that's funny to me! Anyway, Smith wrote a newspaper column for Jackie. On the road, they roomed together in colored boarding houses and ate together in colored restaurants. He did a lot to keep Jackie calm in the face of all that crap they threw at him. And he did something else nobody seems to remember. He was the point man who got the players to insist on integrated hotels and restaurants in Florida.

"But now," the ghost concluded, "you're going to meet a totally different kind of fella. A guy who did some things when he was young that continue to impact all of baseball after his death. When the guys get together—every Thursday, in heaven —he's the one who tells the best stories. Right up until his death."

Chapter 16
Jocko and Effa

"First of all," the ghost said, "we got to go back and make a stop in 1925. When the fog clears, we're going to search for a lost piece of history. Oh, there it is." He pointed into the misty distance. "That's Newark boulevard you see there—it was beginning to transition from a haven of historic mansions to gritty blue-collar houses in a blue-collar city."

Now they were looking at a building where the entrance was fronted by layers of broad, pristine-white steps, giving the structure the look of a museum. The legend sculpted into the brownish brick facade read "Central High School."

"I know this place," the old ballplayer said. "I knew kids who went here when I was coming up. I used to play the outfield against them over at Schools Stadium. I remember one time there was this—"

"—put a sock in it, Jet, we got a schedule to keep. Through that front door, down the hall . . . Now turn right . . . This is the principal's office."

Inside, an academic-looking man was lecturing a skinny kid who was staring at the floor.

The voice of authority was saying, "I know you've done this on purpose. How could you fail the last semester of your senior year with a brain like yours? I know your dad, and I can assure you he won't stand for this. He's an educated man with three kids. You look at me when I speak to you, young man! He's a good man and a good father. What you did here this semester is an insult to him, to me, to this school, and to yourself. Get out of my sight."

The boy lifted his gaze and looked at the principal. He seemed embarrassed, but the gleam in his eyes indicated he knew exactly what he had done.

He left the office and walked down the hall. He paused in front of a row of lockers. Another student was waiting there.

"How did it go?" the other kid asked. "What's he gonna do to you?"

"It was the standard lecture," his friend answered, "but it wasn't as bad as it could have been. He didn't threaten to call my father. I got another year of baseball out of it."

He smiled. "See you this afternoon at practice."

The ghost chimed in. "The boy's name is Sherman Maxwell but his friends call him Jocko. When he was younger, there was a popular vaudeville act featuring a monkey named Jocko. What happened was that Sherman had climbed a tree in the park for a better view of a baseball game nearby. A fly ball was hit directly at him. He held on for dear life with his right hand and made a barehanded catch with the left.

"An old guy down below laughed and said, 'Will you look at that monkey up there! Did you see what that Jocko just did?'

"The nickname stuck," the ghost said, "mostly because the kid much preferred it to Sherman. Remember that name, boy, he's a big part of why you are on this trip. That stop at the principal's office was to show you how much that kid loves baseball.

He just deliberately flunked that exam so that he could play another season of baseball with his teammates at Central.

"And as much as he loves it right now as a kid," Josh added, "he will love it even more for the rest of his life, which will be a long, long time—he won't die until after his 100th birthday. He'll organize and coach a semipro team called the Newark Starlings. He will walk into a Newark radio station called WNJR that's geared toward black music and black commentators and talk his way into his own sports show."

"Well, I knew him quite well," the old ballplayer interrupted. "He interviewed me a couple of times. In Newark, if Jocko put you on his show you were a neighborhood hero.

"When he walked into that station, he became the first black sportscaster in this country. And he had a full-time job at the post office. For all those decades he was on the radio, he never took a penny from any station, just a token fee by his sponsor, the Ballantine Brewery."

The ghost, clearly impatient with delays in his planned schedule, spoke up. "Well, that's all good information, but we got to get back on track. Let's get out of here because we have to fast-forward a lot of years. Jocko will be established as a radio sportscaster the next time you see him. As the first, he became the electronic Jackie Robinson of communications in America.

"Actually," Josh added, "this part of the journey is only about 10 blocks away."

Through the magic window, they were looking at a back room of a newspaper, the Newark Ledger, an airless storage space filled with olive-green metal filing cabinets. It was what newspaper folks called the morgue, a place where useful articles were clipped by hand from daily papers for filing.

Jocko's brother and sister sat at a long table covered with loose newspaper pages. The Maxwell family and their father—

with Jocko the only exception—had for years been the newspaper's archivists of daily life in New Jersey's largest city. But in baseball season, Jocko was a regular visitor to the morgue.

In a radical move for newspapers of the 1930s, the sports editor had granted Jocko permission to write two paragraphs and include a box score for every Newark Eagles game. Before then, black baseball was not covered. Between the newspaper and what had grown to three stations that form his personal network, Jocko Maxwell had become directly responsible for the Eagles' attendance figures, which were among the league's best.

"But you're not making much money for all that work," Jocko's brother Emerson told him.

"Emerson, I'm your brother—how long do you know me? And don't laugh, Bernice. I never asked the stations for a penny. I had my post-office salary. As for the radio, you know if I like a thing, then doggone it, I'm gonna do it."

Years later, surviving players from the Negro Leagues and mid-20th-century newspaper columnists will say that his meticulous record-keeping and his unique broadcasts of Newark Eagles games were major factors in preserving what we know of that exciting era. At that time, almost nothing was printed about them.

"Well, that's nice," said the old ballplayer as he stood directly behind Jocko. "I always liked this guy. I was a Newark kid, and he was the only radio guy who paid attention to us back then. But why did we have to mess around here in the first place?"

"Jet," replied the ghost, "you had the fastest legs in the Negro National League—and they were a lot faster than your brain. If it weren't for Jocko here, nobody today would know who the hell we were. Our record was worse than the bus trips.

But Jocko, and only Jocko, kept track of what we had done and put it on paper. It was the Maxwells, in that little room, who clipped it out and created an archive for the future."

He turned to the boy. "Don't ever forget him. You are going to be our messenger and you need to always remember what he did for us."

Emotion was clearly welling up as Josh went on. "One last thing you got to know," he said. "They have this writers and broadcasters wing up in Cooperstown's Hall of Fame—we've got to be stunned that Jocko ain't in it. But Jocko never cared. He was on his own mission. He let the world know what was going on in places like Ruppert Stadium and Forbes Field and Comiskey Park when the 'other' teams, meaning blacks, took over from the regular tenants. In his way, the part of America that would listen was educated by Jocko all about these black knights of the open road.

"Now we got to get the hell out of here," the ghost said. "I'm running out of time to even be here. I got to show you a pioneer who never threw a pitch, never hit one, and never wore a uniform."

Effa Manley was a beautiful African-American woman who left Philadelphia in the early 1930s for the lure of a magical New York neighborhood called Harlem. This was the home of a shining slice of black renaissance called Sugar Hill. Its music, poetry, and theatrical artists stamped it as an African-American mecca.

Effa was an activist of amazing achievements. She was at the epicenter of the tableau that was about to unfold through the bus window.

After the fog had floated away yet again, they saw a five-story building bearing the sign "L.M. Blumstein." It was a department store, the busiest in Harlem.

"Who are all those people on the street carrying signs?" the boy asked.

"You notice that all those people are colored," Josh told them. "We're in Harlem. They live here, but they can't work in Blumstein's, where they shop. So they're chanting 'Don't shop where you can't work.' The woman who just picked up that sign is named Effa Manley. They'll win primarily because the next day, during the negotiations, Mrs. Manley shocked the whole room."

"You know, Mr. Blumstein," Effa was saying, "we think as much of our young colored girls as you think of your young white girls. But there's no work for them except as maids or prostitutes."

The ghost grinned. "They won the strike."

The boy spoke up. "What does this have to do with baseball?"

"I'll take this one," the old ballplayer said. "I know Mrs. Manley. She and her husband owned the Eagles. I played for them. She helped keep our league alive. She was a lone woman in a world of very tough men. I guess that makes her one of the first real feminists.

"You have to remember, the owners all bankrolled their teams with money they made through the numbers game. Some of them even had other things on their rap sheets. But she held her own against them."

"Well said, Jet," Josh put in. "Her husband, Abe, was the baseball man. Shortly after their marriage, she moved to Newark. Abe had a black team called the Brooklyn Eagles that he moved to Newark and played in the Negro National League.

"Abe liked nothing better than to scout and find players, or make a trade that favored the Eagles. But he hated the business side—so Effa handled that. She truly kept the team's name in front of the community. She held the team purse strings, made opening day a city showpiece where even the white mayor knew he had to show up. She raised money for charity—and she did love baseball. After all, she met Abe at the major leagues' World Series."

"Well," Josh interrupted, "before we move on, I want to show the boy how tough she could be."

He smiled and raised a ghostly eyebrow before opening the story. "They had this league meeting in Chicago. Like I said, the guys who owned these teams were tougher than Josh's old catcher's mitt. So Mrs. Manley gets to talking about promotion and how they got to spend more money and come up with more creative ideas.

"Well, they all groaned. One of them said, 'We don't need to do any of that stuff. We open the gates and they come. Give us a break, Effa.' At which point she began to cry. Cum Posey got so mad that he cursed at her. She sobbed louder. Then one of them, I think it might have been Alex Pompez, said, 'Please don't do that. I hate that. We'll do what you suggested.'

"Effa smiled sweetly and turned off the waterworks as though she had a switch. Later, Cum Posey actually called her and apologized for using profanity."

The ghost's grin broadened. "That was Mrs. Manley. She was a beautiful woman who could smile like she was hitting on you and get you to do whatever you wanted. Or when it came to giving you a raise, that charming smile turned to ice cubes."

"When you get a lot older," the old ballplayer said, smiling at the boy, "you will understand the lesson here."

Fog returned and filled the window. Little by little, the mist faded, and the familiar sight of Ruppert Stadium took up the view.

They were in 1946, and the Eagles were taking batting

practice. The old ballplayer tapped his personal experience to tell the boy more about the Manleys.

"They had a long marriage," he said, "but they were as different as champagne and orange juice. Effa was the hard-boiled businesswoman, the smiling socialite, and the glamorous friend of celebrities like Lena Horne, Cab Calloway, and Joe Louis.

"Abe had patience or interest for none of that. For him, the world was one big, exciting baseball field. He had no politics except those of the infield-fly rule and the intentional base on balls. He scouted with a voracious appetite from one end of New Jersey to the next. From right under his nose, he discovered Monte Irvin in Orange and Larry Doby in Paterson.

"But their partnership was so successful that a number of Negro League clubs studied and tried to emulate the promotional success of the Manleys. One of them, the Baltimore Elite Giants, went a step further. They got permission from Mrs. Manley to play a number of their own home games in Newark because the attendance there was always better.

Josh cut in excitedly, "Look—look out there!" He pointed to the seats just in front of the left-field foul line. Monte Irvin had fouled off three pitches—and a man in a tie and a white shirt was scrambling after the bouncing balls in the stands.

"When the game started," Jet said, "it was Mule Suttles, the home-run-hitting first baseman, who ripped a couple of line-drive fouls into seats just past the Eagles dugout—and that guy was back again, racing the fans for the balls.

"Who is that guy?" the boy asked. The old ballplayer and Gibson laughed. "That's Abe," the grandfather said. "He used to tell us about the cost of baseballs every time he got a chance. He'd get angry if the pitcher asked the umpire for a new ball. And he retrieved a lot of foul balls, chasing them down ahead of a lot of paying fans."

"I don't know if we can tell the boy the most interesting story about Effa," the ghost said. "I mean, given his age and all."

"I know what you're talking about," the old ballplayer answered. "So I'll tell him—I have more common sense than you."

He turned back to the boy. "You've gotta understand that this is meant in no way to put down Mrs. Manley. Like we showed you, she had a powerful role in keeping our league alive, and she was a beautiful and strong-willed woman."

He cleared his throat. "They had this pitcher named Terris McDuffie. In 1938, he went 13-2, primarily because he had a whole variety of pitches. He was a showman who called himself Terris 'The Great' McDuffie because a movie about a baseball player called Elmer the Great was popular that year. Terris even had 'The Great' embroidered on his windbreaker. On top of that, he was a tall, good-looking young man.

"Well, Effa liked him—I don't know exactly how much she liked him, but all the players agreed it was a lot. One day she comes to Ruppert with a couple of girlfriends and tells the manager that she wants him to pitch McDuffie so all her friends can see him.

"'Can't do that,'" says the manager. "'He pitched yesterday.'"

"'Well, I want him to pitch today.'"

"'Can't do that.'"

"'Well, I'm the co-owner and general manager of this team, and you're just the field manager. So you will do it.'"

"'Wrong. I ain't your field manager no more. I quit.'

"So he walks away. He's heading toward the exit when Abe catches him. 'That's ridiculous,' Abe says. 'You pitch who you want. I'll handle Effa.'

"The kicker to this story is that Abe may not have been as naive as he seemed. After the game, he called a team meeting for the next day and announced he has just traded McDuffie to the New York Black Yankees for two broken bats and two old sliding pads. He never explained why."

The ghost turned back to the boy. "We've got one more stop. Just one more. And after that, I got nothing more to tell. The rest"—his arms made a sweeping gesture—"will be up to you."

Chapter 17
An Empty Honor

Josh took a deep sigh and closed his eyes. The old ballplayer stared at him intently. The boy also seemed to sense something important was going on.

They both felt as though the ghost had something to do . . . something he couldn't avoid.

In a very tired voice, Josh said, "Look outside, young man."

The fog seemed frozen in place, almost as though, like Josh, it faced something that it just didn't want to do. And then, it arose like a curtain. Now they saw Ebbets Field in Brooklyn. A night game was in progress. The arc lights illuminated Flatbush like a civic necklace.

"One day," Josh said, interrupting the reverie, "nothing will remain of this . . . Not the ballpark . . . not even the Dodgers. But you will remember the place, you and your grandfather, just as its ghosts will never fade. This is where Jackie Robinson paid the dues that opened the golden gates. I died and you were out of baseball, Jet, before the results were in. But look what he did here, and what Larry Doby did in Cleveland.

"That world out there is the place where Jackie first showed the way from a lead at first or third base that struck fear into the hearts of future Hall of Fame pitchers. And the place where Jackie first showed the way to the emancipation of black ballplayers everywhere.

"That was then. But in the future, it will be gone, all of it: the Dodgers, the baselines, the dugouts, the fences. And, of course, Jackie."

Even Josh didn't know it, but two decades into the future, the steel down below that once was the incredible civic spirit of Ebbets Field will remain forever beneath the concrete and steel intestines of what became a Brooklyn public-housing project.

And over in Manhattan, the same fate awaited the Polo Grounds.

So now they were headed to the future, to a night in 1997 when all of baseball was about to pat itself on the back for letting Jackie Robinson and all the others into their snow-white enclave. There would be no mention of the hundreds they kept out. All of this would be accomplished, of course, without guilt despite more than a century of arrogance.

"Behind that fog," the ghost said, "is a place. A place where you never saw a game, in a world far into the future from this moment. It's only eight miles northwest of Brooklyn but a thousand light-years of history away from when this trip began.

"What you are going to see tonight is a kind of graduate school for the boy after all he has seen with us. He will listen and watch and learn how far we've come. More important, tonight he will learn why we had to go that far in the first place."

Ahead, they could see the lights of Shea Stadium. The ghost had explained that—cosmetically—this was the night all of baseball would seemingly pay its debt to Jackie. But historically, it was an exercise in self-promotion and self-gratification.

Unspoken by the two men was the shared thought that

there was something emotionally off-center about the idea of honoring Jackie Robinson at Shea Stadium in Queens. It wasn't typecasting any more than it was psychic vibrations that brought both the president of the United States and this ceremony to this place. What it was, in fact, was the availability of the only empty theater in town. Certainly these Mets had nothing to do with the old Brooklyn franchise; the Dodgers they would play after these ceremonies were simply transplants out of a Los Angeles Lotus Land, and they had even less to do with Robinson's real team.

The ghostly catcher shattered the silence.

"I know I'm bitter," he said softly, but with urgency beneath. "They wanted me in Cuba and Puerto Rico and Mexico and everywhere else I played—except in my own country. They never wanted me here no matter what my statistics shouted at them. But how in hell do you pay honor to the guy who changed forever the way America finally viewed baseball and race relations when you didn't want him either? Can you really do it by holding your seance in a ballpark where Jackie never played . . . a ballpark that houses a team that didn't even exist back then . . . a ballpark that only served as a kind of spiritual halfway house between the long-gone sites of Ebbets Field and the Polo Grounds?"

Fifty years before, on an April afternoon, Jackie Robinson first walked out of the Ebbets Field clubhouse, up the dugout steps, and into the Brooklyn sunshine, dragging baseball's collective conscience kicking and screaming behind him, all the way into the 20th century.

"Boy," the old ballplayer said to his grandson, "I've often thought that Jackie and, later that season, Larry Doby, saved baseball from itself and its white-supremacy ideas. Fifty years later, here we are in a park that has no ties to Jackie or Brooklyn, half a century from the day he started his journey into a place where no other black man in the modern era of baseball had ever gone. We're here to see a ceremony designed to get them off the hook for what they did to all of us."

"Hell," the ghost broke in, "they're here to pat themselves on the back and say what a good thing they did—when it was their own power structure that kept all of us out. They let us in? Hell, maybe they just got tired of keeping us out. Now they want us to thank the mugger for not hitting us more."

"Look at that scoreboard," the old ballplayer told the boy. "Read how they thank fifteen paid sponsors for this night. Now read the message next to that plastic mural of Jackie rounding third base."

The boy haltingly read aloud: "'He was the handsome, heroic giant of our youth who taught us determination, taught us perseverance and, finally, taught us justice.'"

"Very good. Now read what it says underneath that."

"Well . . . it says 'Budweiser salutes Jackie Robinson.'"

The hurt and anger in the old ballplayer's expression were evident. And in his voice: "They even sold the damn scoreboard," he muttered.

Given the right emotional framework, the winds of Shea Stadium can make the California Santa Ana seem like the exhaling of a small child. In that instant, the gusts off Flushing Bay picked up. It paused for neither baseball's house ads nor the words of the president of the United States and the commissioner of baseball.

As the cold wind refused to spend itself, Josh Gibson did something that was not intended for the old baseball player whose career he had ended at a home plate decades before. And he didn't do it for the young boy whom all his colleagues in the Great Beyond had chosen to keep their memories alive in the world below. He did it strictly for himself, and for decades both alive and dead when he had kept it bottled up within.

Josh stuck his head out of the bus window and shouted the words he had held inside in heaven above the earth for as long as he could remember. He wanted the wind to embrace them and repeat them and hurl them from foul line to foul line in the stadium below:

"Yeah, you did right by him! Twenty-five years ago on another anniversary of the day you let him be the first, he stood on the pitcher's mound with the commissioner of baseball, nearly blinded by the diabetes that would soon kill him. And he told all the pompous dignitaries and the huge crowd that he would be even more pleased if he could just look down and see a black manager wearing a uniform shirt with 'Mets' across its front. He said he'd like to live to see that.

"Nine days later, he was dead.

"It was more than 1,093 days after he died that you finally hired a black manager!" He was screaming now. And the sound mixed with the howling of the wind frightened the boy. "Black managers?" he went on. "What about Gene Baker? Before Robinson, the Pirates let him manage their Class A Batavia farm—and they didn't even give him enough players to finish the season. Have you thought about him?"

His voice spit thunder now as though he were heaving the words at the stadium's image. "Why don't you tell them about the night in Montreal in 1946?" Josh Gibson bellowed. "How two anonymous club owners agreed in private that if Jackie made it from there to the bigs that a situation might arise when a preponderance of Negroes in parks like Yankee Stadium, the Polo Grounds, and Comiskey Park could threaten the resale value of those major-league clubs."

"Why didn't you say what you really thought, you anonymous bastards? Why didn't you say, 'There goes the neighborhood'?

"How many shirts with Jackie's number forty-two will you sell this week?"

The bus grew chillingly still.

In a soft, weary whisper, Josh said, "Sorry about that, Jet. And Jeffy. I'm sorry the boy had to hear me lose my temper like that."

The old ballplayer's face softened. Then he looked at the strange ectoplasm that held his old adversary together. "Don't apologize for that," he said. "You just shouted what I thought."

He paused, lowered his head, gazed back at his friend. "And before we separate, I want you to know that a lot of us thought that you, and not Jackie, should have been the first."

"Cut the bullshit!" Josh retorted heatedly. "You ain't gonna move me! Ghosts can't cry . . . No tear ducts . . . and no reason."

He turned in a formal-seeming way toward Jeffy. "Boy," he said simply, "this trip is over. You are the messenger now. You know the story." He raised his right hand to a "pledge" pose that was also a farewell. "Tell it. Don't let them ever forget us."

The ghost vaporized.

The boy and his grandfather stared at the space where the figure had been. Then at each other. Their 70-year age gap, at that moment, had likewise vaporized—they were united in astonishment.

Jeffy cut the silence with a whisper. "What do we do now, Pop Pop?"

"I don't know, boy." He looked around the vacant bus. "We better get out of here and find a real bus, or something. It's getting dark."

The old ballplayer climbed out. He was limping as badly as he always had since Josh and he tumbled together in Ruppert Stadium decades before. The boy took his hand. They walked until they saw the lights of Ferry Street. The old man slumped down on the steps of Our Lady of Fatima Church.

His leg throbbed fiercely. The pain he felt was, once again, his old enemy and, strangely, his friend. He squinted at the sky through the gathering twilight and shook his fist as another spear shot the length of his leg. Then, as if struggling to return to what had been normal before all of this, he looked up at the twilight and shouted through the pain—six words, the same six words that began his day every day, year after year:

"Damn you, Josh Gibson. Damn you!"

"Stay here, Pop Pop," the boy said, obviously frightened. "I'm going to find someone to help us." He took off running. Ten minutes later, he was back, sitting in a squad car with a policeman.

"Hey, old-timer," the cop said. "Are you OK?"

"Will you take us home?" Jet asked humbly.

"Sure. Can you walk to the car?"

"What time is it?"

"About five thirty."

Five thirty. The Greater Newark Tournament game had been supposed to start at 2:00, when Josh picked them up. All that they had seen . . . the miles and the decades and the milestones . . . and yet they had been gone just five hours. All that, and they were still just five miles from home.

"I'll drive you, old-timer," the cop said genially.

He helped the old ballplayer into the back seat, assisted by the boy. Jeffy sat up front next to the policeman. As they pulled away from the curb, the cop said, "Hey, young man, I got a surprise for you. Understand, I don't do this for everyone."

He punched a button on his dashboard. The siren wailed. The boy laughed and applauded as he saw the red light spinning. But the old man heard none of it. He was lost in thought, and he was a little scared.

"What am I going to tell my daughter?" he thought. "How am I ever possibly going to explain this? How could I do this to her? She'll never let me take the boy anywhere again."

He shook his head. "All these years I've walked like a cripple. Didn't he do enough to me?" Then he threw his head back and said it out loud:

"Damn you, Josh Gibson, damn you. Why couldn't you leave me alone?"

Chapter 18
Cooperstown

The squad car turned onto 13th Street, red light spinning and siren wailing. The narrow street was packed with parked cars on both sides; even double-parking was stymied. The car jumped the curb at a space next to a hydrant and rolled to a stop on the tiny front lawn of Jet's home.

The old ballplayer looked out the window at the people who were standing on porches and front steps trying to see what the commotion was about. He was embarrassed.

The boy jumped out of the police car and ran toward the steps where his mother had opened the door. She must have come in from the hospital an hour or two earlier—underneath her kerchief, her hair was already up in curlers. She wore a faded green bathrobe and her eyes had the look of an avenging demon. The cop stood watching on the lawn.

Effa—his daughter, the boy's mother—was furious. She turned abruptly toward the neighbors and shouted, "Go back inside! This ain't no show. It's just an old man who got lost and got my boy lost, coming home to try to explain how it happened. Go inside and leave us alone!"

The cop approached the front steps. He took his hat off.

"Good evening, ma'am. I just have to be sure they belong here. He says his name is Jefferson, and—"

"—yes, that's his name," she broke in. "He is my father, and right now I'm not sure I want to admit that." She placed a protective arm around the boy's shoulder. "The boy belongs here. But right now I haven't decided about him." She pointed an accusing finger at the old ballplayer.

"Is everything all right?" the cop said quietly.

"Yes, it is, Officer, and I thank you for bringing my boy home. He belongs here. But I have to do some thinking about him." She again pointed at her father.

"Well, then I'll be going." The cop smiled. "I'm sure he has quite a story to tell."

He climbed behind the wheel and slowly backed his car off the lawn. Her son and her father had gone into the front hallway. She followed, and the sound when she slammed the door behind her was a kind of exclamation point that sent the neighbors scurrying back inside.

The three of them stood at the foot of the staircase. She leaned against the polished black wood of the railing. The boy spoke first.

"Oh, Mom, you should have been there! We were traveling in this magic bus with a ghost named Josh Gibson and we went to Mexico and Chicago and . . ."

"Get upstairs, boy," she cut him off. "Go put on your pajamas, brush your teeth, and say your prayers—and they better be good after what the two of you have done to me."

"But, Mom, you don't—"

"—you get upstairs, and I mean now! And you"—she pointed the same scornful finger again at her father—"go into the living room. You got some explaining to do."

He sat meekly on the sofa. She sat across from him in the

old Morris chair that he and her mother had bought before they moved into the house after their honeymoon.

Her chin was propped in her right hand, and her eyes flashed the same angry, hurt look that her mother always had when he had disappointed her. Effa was still a beautiful woman . . . yet, he suddenly understood, not as beautiful as she had been. He realized what the strain of supporting the three of them was doing to her.

"Talk!" she blurted. "Tell me about the nonsense you filled his head with. You heard him, talking about ghosts and magic buses! How could you do this? Are you senile? Maybe you do belong in a home for old folks. Do you know what I went through? No sign of either of you, no note—no idea at all what might have happened! I was crazy with fear."

She broke down and started crying. He stood up, hesitated, then went to her and put his arms around her. He stroked her hair.

"I can't tell you," he said. "I just can't. You wouldn't believe me. And it would only make it worse between us." He bowed his head. "I'll talk to you in the morning."

She shoved his hand away and jumped to her feet. "Don't you even think about talking to me!" She ran up the stairs.

He knew she was furious, but never did he expect what happened the next morning.

He heard his daughter and his grandson in the kitchen. Every time the boy mentioned Josh Gibson, she harshly silenced him. The boy had never seen her like this. Yet he persisted, so she leaned down and shook him. Hurt and puzzled, the boy cried.

The old ballplayer had heard enough. He walked into the kitchen and faced Effa.

"I'd like to explain," he said.

"Not to me!" she said, clearly seething. "It's all I can do to let you live with us. And I'm late for work." She slammed the door behind her.

The silent treatment continued for eight days. Much of the time, Jet and the boy sat in the kitchen and spoke almost in whispers.

"He said I'm the messenger," the boy murmured. "You heard him." He adjusted himself in his seat, sat up straighter. "Where do I start, Pop Pop?"

The old ballplayer had to smile at the question. "Seems to me," he answered, "you'll just know when the time comes. You got a lot of livin' ahead of you. A lot of folk who need to know the story. It's in your hands now. I wouldn't tell your mother that yet. She and I got some fences to repair first."

On the morning of the ninth day, with the boy in school and the mother at work, the grandfather lifted old Martín Dihigo out of the umbrella stand, limped out the door and down the steps, then turned right. He had not been out of the house since the night they returned.

It was a marvelous day, brisk and clear with a perfect splash of sunlight for June. With no plan and no thought in mind, he headed for Abe Siegel's candy store. Somehow, he felt Abe was the link. Abe had suggested a return to Ruppert Stadium with the boy and the Greater Newark Tournament. What was it Abe had said? If you saw ghosts, then they are real, because they are yours. Who can know, he'd said, but you, yourself, what this all means?

Yes, Abe was his bet shot—his only shot. Jet could not figure this out all by himself. By the time he pulled open the worn screen door at the store, he was convinced that Abe would be his Rosetta stone, the key to all he and the boy had seen, the answer to what would come next.

Abe was straightening up a stack of *Star-Ledgers* in the

news rack. The old ballplayer was relieved to see there were no customers. Without speaking, Abe turned back to the counter, poured two cups of coffee. He motioned the old ballplayer to a table. He placed the cups down, wiped his hands across the big white apron he always wore, and sat across from his friend.

"Well, boychik," he began with his customary nickname, "it's been almost 10 days since you took the boy back to Ruppert. So, tell me. What happened? See any ghosts?"

Jet stared for almost a full minute into his companion's dark eyes. "Abe," he started, before pausing again to gaze across the silent store. "I couldn't tell this to anyone else. But to you, I . . . well, Abe, Josh was there. I must have been out of my mind. I let him take the boy and me to places you wouldn't believe . . . all of them in that damn old Newark Eagles bus . . . Alabama . . . Pittsburgh . . . the South Pacific!

"We saw Effa and Abe . . . Dandridge and Irvin . . . Satch and even Paul Robeson. We went to . . . well, before this goes any further"—he sipped coffee, his eyes misty—"am I senile? Am I crazy? Abe . . ." Jet wiped his eyes with a paper napkin. "You gotta help me."

Abe leaned forward, folded his gnarled hands on the table. "Did the boy see them too? Did Josh say why he came for you? Did you find out what he meant by who will tell the children?"

"Yes to all of that," the old ballplayer said as much to himself as to Abe. "He and Satch told the boy, my grandson, he would be the messenger—the one who would make sure future generations would never forget that we had a league and we had our time. And that no matter what they did, they couldn't stop us from playing the game."

"Well, look, Jet." Abe leaned back in his chair and crossed his arms. "I ain't no philosopher. And I sure as hell ain't no ghostbuster. I'm just old Abe Siegel trying to run a candy store in a dying neighborhood in the daytime and trying to fight off my own personal demons when I'm alone in bed at night. I reckon you ain't senile. You saw what you saw, and the boy saw what he saw." He shook his head in dawning wonderment. "Have you seen Josh since you got back?"

"No. And that's why I don't know if this was real or this—"

"—Jet, the boy is your witness. It's in his hands now, this role of messenger. It's like your Eagles and the Newark Bears would say when they fell behind three or four runs in the first inning: Don't panic. Sit back and let the game come to you. Whatever you saw, whatever is expected of you . . . it's gonna come to you and the boy in time. Meanwhile"—he smiled broadly—"drink your coffee and get out of here. I just got three customers over there."

That night after dinner, Effa made the first peace overture. She sent the boy to his room to do his homework, then sat down at the table across from her father.

"Look, you have to understand how you panicked me," she said in an even voice. "George died in Korea. Jeff and you are all I have left. You know I love you—but you got to be more alert about him. You have to be more considerate of me. You can't just take him and go off. I don't wanna hear about ghosts and black baseball players and your bitterness about things I never saw.

"I want to raise my child. And I want you to be here and to think about what's right for him." She paused, looked deeper into his eyes. "Can you do that for me, Daddy?"

She got up, walked over, and kissed the top of his head.

"Daddy" melted him. He knew the war was over.

Things settled down for a while. The old ballplayer watched Yankee games on television with the boy. They walked to the park to play catch. Their lives were reshaping into the way they'd been before the ghosts had come. June morphed into July.

On a mid-July day, they were sitting in the kitchen together. The boy was doing his homework. The old ballplayer was reading the *Star-Ledger* sports section. The radio played softly.

Then the old ballplayer said, "Make that louder, son. The news is coming on."

A voice floated across, from WNJR, the black station: "Well, this is the weekend, the one we've all waited for. Jackie Robinson, the man who broke the major-league color line, will be inducted into the Baseball Hall of Fame up in Cooperstown, New York, on Sunday. And you don't need a ticket. I'll be there. Will you? We owe him that."

Their astonishment grew as they realized the voice belonged to Jocko Maxwell, the man regarded as America's first black sportscaster. Jet and Jeffy stared at each other in silence.

"That's Jocko, Pop Pop!" the boy said in a stunned whisper.

"I know."

"Is it a sign?"

"I don't know." The old ballplayer suddenly stood up. "What I do know is, we got to be there in Cooperstown Sunday."

"But you don't drive! And she—"

"—it's up to you, boy. She'll do it for you."

That night at dinner, the boy tried.

"We could be back Sunday night," he said at the end of his pitch.

"No," she said firmly.

"Please! It's important to Pop Pop and me."

"He told you that?"

"No! I told him that."

She turned to the old ballplayer. "You behind this?"

"Are you calling the boy a liar?" he retorted.

Jeffy cut in. "Please, Mom?"

"I don't know." She shook her head. "This is getting too important to you. And I don't know why. I don't want to talk about it anymore. I'm sorry, but I'm going to bed."

The old ballplayer and the boy watched her go, heard her door close.

"Why won't she let me explain about the ghost?" Jeffy said. "Then maybe she'd understand why we have to go."

"She's a little afraid," Jet replied. "And I can't blame her. I mean, how would you feel if someone told you about a ghost you didn't know anything about, or even believe in? Thinking about it that way . . . I'm still not sure it happened."

"Well," Jeffy said in as strong a voice as he could muster, staring hard at his grandfather, "didn't they say I am supposed to be the messenger?"

Jet gazed back at him. Then a big smile spread across his face. "Listen, boy. I . . . I'm still confused, but I have a feeling it wasn't an accident that we heard Jocko. I have a feeling that Cooperstown holds the answer. Your mom is upset now. You try again in the morning."

He didn't have to.

For some reason, without warning, the next morning she walked into the kitchen and made an announcement.

"I've been thinking about this," Effa said carefully. "I don't know exactly why, but . . . it's important to the both of you, so I suppose we could go. If we left early and drove back right after the ceremony. I guess I could pack us a lunch, and . . ." She sighed as though in surrender. Then her voice shifted. "But here's the rules—and I mean it. If either of you gets more than five feet away from me, we are going straight back home whether Jackie has spoken or not. You hear me? I'm not playing about this."

Then Effa caught herself whispering to no one in particular: "I sure would like to see Jackie. He sure was a fine-lookin' man."

On induction day each year, the town is packed. Across from the museum a U.S. Postal Service trailer sells canceled Hall of Fame postage stamps as keepsakes. A number of eateries and baseball souvenir stores line Main Street, leading up to the Hall itself. They used to hold the ceremonies in front of the red-bricked Hall of Fame's lawn, but the crowds got so large they moved it to a spacious municipal park called the Clark Sports Center Park.

Cooperstown was not a place that attracted Negro Leaguers. None of his fellow players were enshrined at the site, and until Robinson broke the line, there'd been no hope that any of them ever would be. A few memorabilia stores flanked the building, and the boy was fascinated by the window displays.

"We best move along and find a place," the old ballplayer told his family. "I'd like to get close enough to hear."

The Hall of Famers in attendance sat in straight-back chairs behind the dais. Each wore a yellow sports jacket. The commissioner of baseball walked to the microphone to introduce Jackie.

"That's Ford Frick," the old ballplayer whispered to his grandson. "You remember when we heard Stanley Woodward, the newspaper editor, push him into backing Jackie when the Cardinals wanted to strike? He did that out of fear, not out of conviction."

"Daddy," Effa said, "hush. Jackie's getting ready to speak."

Jackie Robinson stepped up to the microphone. He stood

there silently for a moment, his facial features communicating a mixture of joy and sadness. Faint strands of gray had begun to creep into his hairline. The slight hint of a stenosis at the juncture of his neck and back served as a reminder that nothing is forever—even heroes. He was forty-three years old. Five years earlier, he had retired from baseball after he was traded to the Giants. The Dodgers were leaving Brooklyn for California. But Jackie's baseball heart wouldn't let him leave Flatbush.

Then he spoke.

"Thank you very much, Mr. Frick. First, let me say how much of a thrill it is to be coming into the Hall of Fame with the other new inductees, Bob Feller, Bill McKechnie, and Edd Roush. I want to also let you know that I feel quite inadequate here this morning. But I think a lot of this has been eliminated, because today, it seems that everything is complete.

"First of all, I want you to know that this honor that was brought up on me here could not have happened without the great work and the advice and guidance that I've had from three of the most wonderful people that I know. And if any of them weren't here today, I know that this day could not be complete. But they're all here. And I just hope you don't mind if I just pay a word of thanks and a tribute to my adviser and a wonderful friend, a man who I consider a father, Mr. Branch Rickey.

"And my mother, who taught me so much of the important things early in life. I appreciate no end, my mother, Mrs. Robinson. And lastly, ladies and gentlemen, my wife, who has been such a wonderful inspiration to me. And the person who has guided and advised me throughout our marriage. I couldn't have been here today without her help."

As Robinson spoke, the old ballplayer began to shake. He put an arm over the boy's shoulder to steady himself.

"And then I . . . and I must thank the baseball writers . . . I never thought at all that I would have this wonderful honor coming to me so early in my lifetime. And to have the writers elect me on the first time is a thrill that I shall never forget."

The old ballplayer was crying. Rivers of tears slid down his cheeks.

"We have been up on Cloud Nine since the election. I don't ever think I'll come down. But I want to thank all of the people throughout this country who were just so wonderful during those trying days. I appreciate it at no end, and it's the greatest honor any person could have, and I only hope that I'll be able to live up to this tremendously fine honor.

"It's something that I think those of us who are fortunate, again, must use in order to help others. Because it's such a tremendous honor that we should be able to go out and do things to help. I'm just grateful and I'm sorry I've taken so long, but I just wanted to you know that I appreciate it so much. Thank you."

The old ballplayer was sobbing. He could not stop thinking about all the history that preceded this moment. Tears streamed down his face, and after the end of the speech they continued. His daughter reached for her father's other hand. They turned to go, but the old man limped his way around a left turn onto Main Street. The old ballplayer, a hand on his grandson's shoulder, said quietly through his tears, "I just wish the guys were here to see this."

"But they are, Pop Pop!" the boy said excitedly. "They're walking right in front of us—Josh and Satch and Leon Day! Can't you see them?"

And then the sky turned coal black, and a tremendous clap of thunder seemed to freeze them in place. A jagged spear of lightning cut through the darkness and slammed against the Hall of Fame roof a block away. A burst of sunlight seemed to explode through a crease in the darkness. Main Street Cooperstown is only two blocks, but the unmistakable laughter of Josh Gibson echoed down its length, followed by the sound of Jeffy's excited voice shouting:

"Mommy, mommy! Pop Pop isn't limping anymore."

END

Acknowledgments

Five players from the Negro National and the Negro American Leagues provided the historical anecdotes in this book through interviews that took thirteen years. They were Larry Doby, Monte Irvin, Ray Dandridge, Max Manning, Buck O'Neil, plus Effa Manley, general manager of the Newark Eagles. Others who helped unravel the mysteries of a way of life long gone include the Yankees' Phil Rizzuto, who recalled his trauma as a high school teenager when he faced the great Satchell Paige; Bill White, a Black major leaguer who became President of Major League Baseball's National League; my running buddy, Charles Mintz, who later became a rabbi and who earlier learned, along with me, how to sneak into Newark's Ruppert Stadium.

And, perhaps most of all, one patient, anonymous older gentleman who told a kid who the Eagles were on the day he was surprised to see them in Ruppert Stadium when he had come expecting to see the all-White Triple-A Newark Bears. He told me to stick around, because these were the unrecognized heroes Major League Baseball's racism had barred.

And then there was my dad, Harry Izenberg, a failed minor league baseball player, who taught me to love the game no matter who played it. Between their guidance, I often became the only white kid in short pants in the joint when the Eagles played.

Bob Izenberg, who, as usual, atoned for my computer ignorance.

The cover photos were provided as the property of the Baseball Hall of Fame in Cooperstown, N.Y.

About the Author

Jerry Izenberg, columnist emeritus at the New Jersey *Star-Ledger*, has been inducted into eighteen Halls of Fame and is winner of the coveted Red Smith Award—the highest honor given by the Associated Press Sports Editors. He and his wife, Aileen, live in Henderson, NV and have four children, nine grandchildren, and three great grandchildren.

This is his sixteenth book and second novel.

More By Admission Press

Looking for your next great read?
Visit www.admissionpress.com